WOLF DUKE

MEDIEVAL WOLF KINGS #1

NICOLA DAVIDSON

WOLF DUKE © Nicola Davidson
First Edition: July 2024
ISBN: 978-0-473-71477-2
Country of Production: New Zealand
Cover: Dar Albert at Wicked Smart Designs
Editor: Mackenzie Walton

PROLOGUE

In ancient times lived the Titaness Leto, companion of Zeus and mother of Apollo and Artemis. Some say she was a shapeshifter who could assume wolf form. Others speak of an unbreakable bond after wolves guided a desperate mother and her newborns to the river Xanthos to drink and bathe. Leto is revered for her strength and courage against her vengeful enemy, Hera, and to this day is worshiped alongside her divine twins by wolves everywhere.

———

Ashcross Castle, The Eastern Lands, England
Summer 1475

"*Y*ou're not frightened we are being stalked, my love?" Hugo's amused words danced in her mind through their bonded link, but Magdalena de Wynter,

Queen of the Eastern Lands and Alpha Female of the de Wynter gray wolf pack, didn't so much as glance at her beloved mate as they strolled in human form through the lush and fragrant castle gardens. No, not by a twitch would the four precious cubs following them know their thumping paws, swishing tails, and excited snorts could be heard a mile away.

Learning to hunt was a rite of passage, and no wolf started with skill and stealth.

"*I am terrified,*" she returned huskily. "*Surely the only remedy is taking me back to bed.*"

"*You are insatiable, madam,*" Hugo growled, the low, rasping tone licking at her senses like a caress.

"*Yes. Just like my mate,*" said Magdalena, almost moaning as she recalled the masterful way he had pleasured her earlier, while dawn cast golden rays over the tempestuous North Sea. Hugo was a magnificent lover.

In truth, he was a magnificent everything. King. Mate. Father. Someone that a baseborn outcast like herself might dream about, but never hope to meet, let alone rule alongside. Hugo was far too important. Not only did he rule the Eastern Lands as anointed king, but he was also keeper of the Book of Lore, the powerful ancient tome that held a complete history of English Wolfdom. No scribe touched it; the births and deaths, battles, ceremonies and laws merely appeared. Legend said the Book had been a gift from Leto herself to recognize the service and bravery of the first Wolf King, and that the flawless ruby-studded lock was in fact blood drops from Apollo and Artemis. From the Book's constant green glow and low hum, Magdalena would believe it. Whoever held the Book of Lore not only held the Eastern Lands, but knowledge beyond time.

What was entirely *unbelievable*: how she and Hugo had met.

One fateful day in a busy tavern where she toiled in the kitchens preparing food, she'd been lured out of her corner by an exotic, heady scent. *His* scent, calling to her like a Siren. As soon as she'd laid eyes on the rugged, fair-haired stranger, the air had snapped and crackled as they'd both pushed through the crowd to reach each other. Then, as Leto decreed when souls recognized their fated mate, her body began preparing itself: the strange tingle at the nape of her neck, the relentless, aching throb between her legs.

Naturally, Magdalena knew of rutting. Wolves indulged their carnal urges without shame, and while it was pleasant enough, she'd always wanted something more. Most males said she was too proud and contrary, certainly too old to find her fated mate. Then she'd met Hugo and discovered the true wanton within. Even more unexpectedly for a mature and seemingly barren wolf, years after their mating ceremony, she'd experienced her first breeding heat. Wolf coupling was often rough and raw, but how they had survived such a fierce onslaught of unquenchable lust, she would never know. This was why those with wolf blood could only breed with their fated mate; they would kill a human with such need and the knotting that made them one. But Magdalena had conceived, and two months later birthed a most yearned-for litter: rare princesses Evaine, Isabel, and Cecily, and Prince Lucan, the heir. To be a mother was a joy beyond words, even if her cubs were the noisiest, messiest, hungriest little beasts in the realm. After initially treating her with grave suspicion, the de Wynter pack now spoke her name with reverence. Finally, Magdalena belonged somewhere.

Every wish had come true. Because of Hugo.

"I humbly thank thee, my queen. For those memories and all your gifts," said her mate, the praise warming her like a cloak in winter. *"It shall be my honor and pleasure to show you how much. But first, we must play the game. Only after the cubs have startled us with their skill will I permit you to retire to your solar for...hmmm, rest and refreshment."*

Magdalena swallowed hard. The way he loved her was quite astonishing, except it was far more than that. He treated her as his equal. They did everything together: hunt, fight, play, and rule over the vast expanse of the Eastern Lands, which stretched from Hadrian's Wall near the Scottish border, all the way down to Oxford and across to the North Sea. Although they had several estates, their principal residence, Ashcross Castle, was a stone fortress about twenty miles outside of Norwich. Other packs ruled the remaining three quarters of the realm: the Armstrongs over the Northern Lands, Hawthorns over the Southern Lands, and Beaumonts over the Western Lands.

"I swear I'll be the most startled mother in England," she replied, attempting a meek tone and only managing teasing.

Hugo growled again, his unwavering lust for her flooding their bonded link. But moments later, a large shrub rustled like it was trying to shed every leaf, and their fearless firstborn, Evaine, sprang from the greenery to land beside them with a heavy thud.

Magdalena gasped, then pressed a hand to her chest as three more cubs followed, each louder than the last. "Goddess!"

Evaine prowled around them in a circle, ears pricked and tail up in triumph. "HA! We have you now," she announced, her voice an endearing blend of high-pitched human child and low wolf growl. As Evaine matured from cub to wolfling to full grown, her voice would eventually settle into the rough rasp of adults, but for now, Magdalena adored the proof her young were still young.

"We do!" giggled Isabel, their sweet secondborn. "Mother and Father must pay a forfeit. What say you, Cecy?"

"More books," said Cecily, their scholarly thirdborn, and the other cubs groaned.

Lucan, the baby of the litter, and by far the most mischievous, rolled his eyes. "*Honey cakes*, Cecy. That was the plan. We capture the king and queen for honey cakes."

Hugo cleared his throat. "We shall pay your forfeit..."

The cubs cheered.

"However," their father continued sternly, "Lucan, you must tread softly. Lift those paws. Isabel, no jests while stalking—prey will not fall to laughter. Cecily, I know you are excited to learn, but that tail twitch reveals your position too readily. And Evaine, temper your courage with caution before leaping. Be sure your prey is truly vulnerable and not foxing you."

"Yes, Father," they chorused, but plainly their minds were wholly on the prospect of spiced cakes drizzled with honey.

Magdalena sighed wistfully. While their young were not yet wolflings and still some way before full grown, they were definitely no longer babes. Once upon a time they had loved cuddling into Mother to be groomed; now they wiggled and hopped and twitched their ears, impatient to run and play. Yet they were still small enough to think honey cakes a great treat, and she would cling to these last remnants of cub life. Far too soon for her peace of mind they would leave the pack to search for their fated mate, a difficult and often fruitless quest, but even more so for royalty. Between the assassins, the brigands, and the smooth-tongued charlatans...

No. She would not ponder that. Not on such a glorious summer's morning.

"A moment for me, then honey cakes," said Magdalena as she reached down, unable to stop herself smoothing each cub's fur and scratching behind their ears. They were just so adorable.

"Mo-*ther*," grumbled Lucan, narrowing his green de Wynter eyes in such a Hugo way that she almost laughed. There was certainly no denying their sire.

Hugo tilted his head, his eyes glinting. "Be grateful the queen loves you so, cub. If I had my way—"

"My king. *MY KING*!"

They all froze as a sentry sprinted toward them, his human face flushed and drenched in sweat, and green-and-white de Wynter livery flapping. Then he fell to one knee in front of Hugo.

"Take a breath," said Hugo calmly. "What news?"

"The Book of Lore," gasped the sentry. "It is gone."

Shock rocked Magdalena back on her heels. Impossible! The Book had its own chamber, rested under a glass dome, and was guarded night and day with a six-hourly change. "How can that be? Who was posted to guard duty?"

The younger wolf met her gaze unflinchingly. "Lord Guy, my queen. He is also...missing...along with two other guards."

She frowned in confusion, struggling to understand the unfathomable words. "You mean they were abducted? Surely there would be a ransom."

"No. Lord Guy rode out with his accomplices. The stablehands who saw them were knocked unconscious and dragged to an unused antechamber. They were only recently found."

Magdalena shuddered, crushed by shame. Guy Saville was her cousin and only living relative, another outcast who had been warmly welcomed by Hugo. As kin to the queen, Guy had received every comfort, every freedom of the castle...and repaid that generosity with the worst possible treachery. How had she been so deceived by his courtly gestures and charming smiles that she'd not seen his true heart: a wolf coveting great power?

"When was Guy last seen?" Magdalena whispered.

"Dawn, my queen," said the sentry grimly.

Hugo snarled, a feral sound of great fury, and the four cubs shrank against Magdalena. Even they understood the grave news, but were struggling to reconcile it with an uncle who had juggled apples and worn oversized shoes to amuse them.

"Noon approaches," bit out her mate, as his fingers clenched around the elaborately carved hilt of his sword. "He's six hours ahead. I'll summon the standing army, every wolf who can be spared, until the Book of Lore is returned. It cannot remain in evil hands. For Guy to wield such ancient power, a power he does not understand—*look out!*"

Magdalena almost screamed as a longbow arrow sailed over their heads and plunged into the grass mere feet away. Such precision over a high castle wall was only possible for a wolf. A human wouldn't have the strength or sight. "Cubs! Behind me!"

Her young scrambled to obey, whimpering in fear.

NICOLA DAVIDSON

Then Evaine peered hard at the arrow. "Mother, there is parchment attached!"

Hugo strode across the gravel path to the arrow, yanking it from the ground and carefully unrolling the paper encircling the shaft and secured with a dab of hot wax. Moments later, he went ashen, before tearing the note to pieces.

Magdalena gasped. Never had her mate looked thus, both enraged and anguished.

Very, very tentatively, she reached out through their bonded link. "*What message, my king?*"

He scowled. "*Guy has raised an army to challenge my crown. If I surrender swiftly, I, and my cubs, will not be imprisoned and tortured, but executed respectfully. He may spare your life, but you'll no longer be Queen of the Eastern Lands or Alpha Female of the pack.*"

Magdalena's stomach roiled, and she pressed a closed fist to her mouth to stop herself retching. Guy dared threaten her beloved mate? Her miracle cubs? No. Guy would seize control of the Eastern Lands over her dead carcass. While there was breath in her body, she would fight him. But first, she had to get the cubs to safety. With a different enemy, the castle would be a sanctuary. However, Guy knew every hidden entrance. Every tunnel. Every staircase and tower. Her cousin had asked enough questions, damn his eyes.

Magdalena turned to the sentry. "Fetch my ladies and four of the strongest warriors. Their only duty will be to protect the princesses and prince until this enemy is vanquished. Do what you can to disguise them. But it must be now."

He glanced at Hugo. "My king?"

8

Hugo nodded curtly. "Do as your queen commands. Then sound the bell. We are at war."

The sentry bowed and ran toward the Great Hall.

"Father, no!" pleaded Evaine. "Do not send us away. We can fight!"

"I'll kill them all!" said Lucan, his eyes wide and jaw trembling.

"Please, Mother," whispered Isabel, as she rubbed her muzzle against Cecily's. "We aren't ready to go alone."

Magdalena fell to her knees, gathering her cubs close as best she could and nuzzling their heads, her heart already shattering at what this day could mean. "My sweet, precious young. I know you have your sire's great courage and daring, but you must stay far away from this battle-field. And you will be protected."

"Why can't you come with us?" asked Cecily, her tail swishing wildly.

"I fight at my mate's side," she replied simply. "That is what it means to be queen. Together. Always."

Evaine shuddered and tried to burrow closer. "What if... what if Uncle Guy wins the battle? He does have the Book of Lore."

Pure icy fear trickled down Magdalena's spine. Indeed, in a fair fight she would wager on Hugo and his warriors every time. But if Guy's black heart unleashed the book's power for evil purposes...not even the gods could save them. "He does, my daughter. That is why you must change to human form and leave. We will come for you at battle's end and eat honey cakes until our bellies groan. Also know this: as long as there are stars in the sky, your father and I will love each of you."

"But it hurts to change," whimpered Isabel. "We hate it."

Magdalena's heart twisted. The more cubs and wolflings changed, the easier the process became. However, because it was so very painful for cubs, she'd been lax in insisting they practice. This day, it was essential they change. In human form, her young could pass for children of perhaps eight or nine summers. That would gift them time.

Helplessly, Magdalena exchanged a glance with Hugo, who abruptly knelt and encircled them all in his massive arms. "Here, now, why all the fuss about changing and hiding for a while? 'Tis only a battle. Have I ever been defeated?"

"No," said Lucan, puffing out his little chest. "You're the greatest king ever. Come, sisters. I know a hollowed tree in the forest that the traitor will never find us, and in human form, we'll all fit. You'll feel foolish at supper for being so scared."

Hugo ruffled Lucan's fur. "I know you'll make me proud, son. But remember everything I've taught you. Be cautious. Tread softly. Keep still and alert. Now go. May Leto and her divine twins bless and keep you all."

And with that, after one last, lingering look, their four cubs bounded away.

Magdalena swallowed an anguished sob. Why did it feel like she would never see her young again?

"My queen..." said Hugo, rising to his feet and holding out his hand. "I must away to the armory. The warriors need guidance, to know the truth of what they face. But if you wish to flee with our cubs...I understand. Guy may spare you."

She hissed. "I shall not spare him. And if it is not my sword that ends his life...I beseech Leto, may it be the sword of my young. Guy will rue the day he challenged my mate and my pack. I am Magdalena de Wynter, Queen of the Eastern Lands, and this I vow."

"Then let us fight how we love," said her mate, his gaze humbling her with the depth of feeling as he laced their fingers. "Together."

"Together, my king," said Magdalena, squeezing his hand. "Always."

CHAPTER
ONE

Eltham Palace, London, Christmastide 1485

I f it weren't for the humans, he would like this castle very much.

Alaric Dafydd Beaumont, King of the Western Lands and Alpha Male of the Beaumont gray wolf pack, glanced approvingly at the red brick palace as he guided his black stallion over the moat's stone bridge.

Truthfully, what he envied most was the palace's thousand acres of prime hunting land. Even in the frigid cold of late December his senses were drowning in the scent of deer, and he yearned to change to wolf form and feast. But no. That wasn't the purpose of his visit. As a landowner of significant means, he'd been invited to celebrate Christmastide with—and swear fealty to—the new human king, Henry Tudor. Known as Henry VII, the Welshman had won his crown the old-fashioned way, defeating the unlucky Richard III at Bosworth Field in August. After being crowned at the end of October, Henry then declared his reign began the day *before* the battle, making everyone on the opposing side a traitor.

Alaric snorted as he smoothly dismounted within the Great Court, slung both traveling satchels over his massive shoulders, then handed the reins to his young squire, Wesley. While wolves were certainly dangerous, vicious, and cunning foes, humans were not far behind. If they lived longer and possessed more than a fragile collection of skin and bones easily felled by a simple cut, bad ale, or wet hair, he might even dread them. But having to pledge 'fealty' to someone with no idea of who—or what—he really was remained infuriating, and it was all due to Hera's spite.

Leto had defeated the queen of the gods, and birthed her divine twins Apollo and Artemis. However, Hera had immediately struck back with two eternal decrees: first, that wolf shifters were forbidden to reveal themselves to humans. Second, wolf kings must forever publicly submit to the human ruler of their realm, a truly grievous insult. Gah. He could almost see Hera's scornful glee as she spoke of *Leto's dogs* kneeling to their *master*. But if any wolf king failed to obey, he and his subjects would be cursed. Death, plague, famine, thrones snatched by usurpers...

Alaric winced. Many claimed it was mere coincidence that King Hugo and Queen Magdalena had been murdered and their four cubs lost just a few years after failing to re-pledge fealty to Edward IV when he regained the English throne. But in Alaric's mind, Hera's evil hand was clear in Guy Saville's victory and the sole reason for journeying to London as human kings came and went. To do otherwise was far too dangerous. Besides, it was only a few days, then he could return to Blackstone Castle, his remote and sprawling estate in the Welsh Marches.

"Brother King."

At the low hail, Alaric smiled as Ranulf Armstrong, King of the Northern Lands, approached. The lean, scholarly gray wolf was an expert apothecary and ruled all past Hadrian's Wall. Unfortunately, in the managing of both Lowland and Highland wolves, he rarely knew peace; Ranulf often jested he would search for his fated mate the moment his subjects behaved. Apart from Alaric's own pack, the wry, humorous, deceptively deadly Scot was one of the few wolves he would trust with his life.

"Brother King," said Alaric, briefly embracing Ranulf and touching foreheads in the manner of affectionate respect. "What news from the North?"

"Aye, the usual," grumbled Ranulf. "James III is a feckless, witless human who will certainly be overthrown by his son afore long. And whether human or wolf, Lowlander and Highlander cannot even drink ale without drawing swords. How fares the West?"

"The Welsh are emboldened by the rise of the Tudors, but what is won in battle can easily be lost. Henry is very, very fortunate that Lord Stanley turned for him. And that his mother is relentlessly ambitious," said Alaric.

"Margaret is a formidable woman indeed. But it would behoove them all to treat Elizabeth of York kindly when she weds Henry. His claim is weak; 'tis her bloodline that legitimizes the throne. I'm not at all certain the Civil Wars are over."

"Peace still seems a great distance away," Alaric agreed.

Ranulf sighed irritably. "It chafes my hose that we must tolerate all this human foolishness with everything else. Hera's vengeance is truly diabolical; forcing us royal wolves to disguise our age or one day pretend to be our own son because we live so much longer. Humans have one strength: they are plentiful. Imagine the wolf population if we could breed all year, without a fated mate. And they just replace dead queens...oh, Goddess forgive me. I meant no pain to you, my friend. I'm sure Theda dances among the stars with our revered ancestors."

Alaric clenched his jaw and glanced down at the faded, slightly ragged royal mating mark etched under his left wrist. His dead mate was a delicate topic, but not for the reason Ranulf believed. Those stormy years with Theda were painful to recall.

Truthfully, he'd not been entirely sure about her, but after a night of revelry, he'd woken with a pounding head, inflamed wrist, and a naked Theda in his arms, sporting an identical mark on her nape. To this day he remembered nothing, yet Theda had explained in great detail all the ways he'd taken her and the marks did prove they were fated mates. However, as soon as she was crowned queen, everything changed. While she adored the jewels, fine clothing, and presiding over banquets and jousts, Theda merely *endured* him. There had been no affection, no desperate lust. She'd kept her own rooms, rarely joined him to hunt, and claimed other duties when he met with dignitaries. On the one occasion he'd questioned their lack of bonding link, Theda had furiously told him his cold nature prevented it.

That was true. He *was* cold. Not overburdened by anger, joy or fear, the reason he often judged disputes or undertook difficult diplomatic missions. But still, he couldn't discard the feeling that a fated mate should rouse *something* in him. Possessiveness? Need? Even love? And surely their passing would be a crushing blow, like five summers ago when his sire had risen to the stars and Alaric reluctantly inherited the Western Lands.

Theda's unexpected death in the spring—falling down stairs after visiting her soothsayer—had not broken him. Perhaps one had to be whole to break. But knowing he would never sleep entwined with his mate, never collapse in ecstatic exhaustion at the end of her breeding heat, never stand guard while his cubs were born, watch them frolic or teach them to hunt...it just made the sky seem grayer. The wind so much icier. Life as a solitary wolf stretched bleakly ahead of him; his eventual death wouldn't bring peace but commence a battle between his cousins to inherit.

An even bleaker thought.

"I know you meant no pain, brother," Alaric said abruptly. "Do not dwell upon it. But we should continue to the Great Hall, lest the humans think we plot rebellion. Has Darius arrived?"

"Yes. Our brother king is inspecting Henry's armory," said Ranulf with a grin. "I just pray Darius conceals the fact he owns tenfold more weapons. Humans like to believe they hold the most treasure."

Alaric nodded. Darius Hawthorn, King of the Southern Lands, was Wolfdom's supreme warrior, only content either planning battles or fighting them. He was a fiercely loyal friend...and a brutal, merciless enemy. Darius had never forgiven himself for arriving too late to assist the de Wynters; since then he'd attacked the usurper on several occasions but succumbed to the Book of Lore's power each time. They now knew only the true blooded heir could reclaim the Eastern Lands...but Lucan de Wynter was nowhere to be found.

"Speaking of treasure," Alaric said, as they crossed the cobbled courtyard toward the magnificent Great Hall, "I hear the bounty on each de Wynter has increased. Ten sacks of gold."

Ranulf's eyes flashed. "Saville is desperate. That scum knows if the cubs survived, they would be full grown now. If the princesses find their fated mates and Prince Lucan returns...the deaths of Saville and his accomplices won't be swift. Or merciful. The River Yare will run red."

"The cubs survived," said Alaric firmly. "We would sense the end of the de Wynter line. Goddess knows how, but they are alive somewhere. I just pray they find sanctuary before the mercenaries find them."

They exchanged a grim glance. While royal wolves could only die of old age or beheading by a pure silver blade, endless suffering could be inflicted. Usually, healing came swiftly, especially in human form. But when severely weakened they remained in wolf form, the healing process became slower and slower, resulting in agony.

Alaric's fists clenched. His sire had grieved for weeks over the murder of Hugo and Magdalena, and sent out countless search parties for the cubs. Since inheriting, Alaric had done the same. But ten full summers had passed. Hope was indeed dwindling.

"Leto keep them safe," said Ranulf, touching his heart. "I suppose we must meet Henry now. I hear conflicting tales...some say he is amiable, others say secretive and wary. But if he is scholarly, perhaps we may have something in common...Goddess, this Great Hall is impressive. Humans can build as well as wolves, I'll concede them that."

They truly could. Eltham Palace's hall was near-new, one hundred feet long and over thirty feet wide. Tall, arched windows allowed plentiful light, rich tapestries lined the walls, and the soaring oak hammerbeam roof was a marvel of construction. Few places made a wolf feel small, but this one succeeded.

As Alaric and Ranulf approached the entrance, four Yeoman of the Guard stepped forward to bar their way.

"State your business," said one, albeit visibly gulping as he studied the size of the two guests. The guard was right to be afraid; either wolf could end his life with a single claw swipe.

Alaric bestowed his diplomatic smile. "Sir Alaric Beaumont of the Welsh Marches and Sir Ranulf Armstrong of the Scottish Marches, here by invitation. We come in peace to swear fealty to Henry VII, king by the grace of God."

The words almost stuck in his throat, but the guards swiftly stepped aside and nodded respectfully.

"You're expected," said the guard. "Welcome to Tudor land."

Alaric and Ranulf exchanged an amused glance. London belonged to Darius.

"Thank you," said Alaric politely.

Leto help them. Two days surrounded by humans would indeed be the longest of his life.

———

The Welsh Marches

For the first time in her life, Princess Evaine de Wynter truly wished for death.

Presently huddled in a tiny, dark, and pungent underground fox den, she didn't even have the strength for a mournful howl. It was far too cold for that, so cold that the tears dripping from her eyes were freezing on her matted fur. Occasionally her stomach growled, but in truth, hunger was a sharp, constant ache now. While a wolf could survive without eating for a fortnight after a large kill, she couldn't recall the last time she'd feasted. Her stomach hurt constantly, never sated on the foraging diet of leaves and berries, small freshwater fish, and the occasional unlucky rabbit that stumbled across her path. She was too weak to hunt. Too weak to flee. Most recently she'd lost the ability to change to human form. If she left this den, the mercenaries that had nearly caught her in Bewdley would find her and drag her all the way back to the Eastern Lands to be murdered by Guy Saville, the way he'd murdered Mother and Father.

Ten years, she'd been running. Ten years of barely evading capture by changing her name and appearance and village each month, living among the humans as a filthy, poverty-stricken widow to keep herself and others safe. But she was weary to the bone. Utterly consumed by grief. And lonely.

So very, very lonely.

Of the two warriors who had spirited her away from Ashcross Castle, one had been killed by mercenaries inside a tavern where he'd gone to purchase ale. The other had eventually fled after a few sword fights, saying she wasn't worth his life. As for the two ladies, one had unexpectedly found her fated mate during their journey, a brief ray of sunshine in the gloom, and Evaine had wistfully wished her well. The other remained at Evaine's side for eight summers, but as an elder, her destined time came to rise to the stars. Evaine had sobbed as she bid her companion a final farewell with all the flowers she could gather. Yet from then on, she became a lone wolf.

Everything was worse when alone in unfamiliar lands. The cold. The dark. The shadows. The screams.

However, there were times she might have sworn Mother appeared in a clearing or across a stream, urging her on. Or that she felt Father's heavy paw on her shoulder, holding her back from revealing herself to enemies. But she'd never seen or sensed the spirit presence of her sisters and brother; the sole reason she believed them to be alive. This gave her a little solace, a tiny tendril of hope that one day they might be reunited. Yet after spending every waking hour with Isabel and Cecily and Lucan as cubs, their long absence from her life was far worse than hunger pangs. The ache was an abyss in her soul.

The sudden snap of a twig outside robbed her of breath. A predator? Or merely nature succumbing to snow?

Evaine peered through the tangle of brambles that concealed the den, her heart pounding.

Goddess. It was that silver-haired female again!

Yesterday at around noon, the warmly dressed, ruddy-cheeked elder wolf had placed food on a nearby tree stump, trying to coax her out. Evaine hadn't dared emerge, knowing full well the danger of poison and how a cunning enemy would use a seemingly sweet elder to lure her into the open. But the scent of roasted mutton and buttered carrot and turnip had been sheer torment, and today she feared the last of her resistance would crumble.

The female cleared her throat. "Good morrow," she began, her voice low yet urgent. "My name is Blanche. I know not why you hide—or who you hide from, but I cannot let you starve or freeze. Please let me help you. It is Christmastide. If you must leave, I can bring supplies. Food. Ale. A woolen blanket or warm cloak. Tonics or poultices if you are injured. If you can stay...I beg you, accompany me to the castle. My master the king is a generous host and I swear on my mate's life that no harm would befall you."

The king?

More tears filled Evaine's eyes, almost blinding her. The

21

humans in Bewdley had warned that the frightening, haunted Blackstone Castle was less than five miles away, but with her senses impaired due to exhaustion and hunger, she'd never found the right direction. Dare she trust this stranger? For if the female spoke true and escorted her to the ruler of the Western Lands, there was no question Princess Evaine de Wynter would be granted sanctuary. The other wolf kings had regarded her sire as a brother.

"You serve King Cyrus?" Evaine croaked, her voice rusty from disuse. Fortunately, only other wolves could hear her speak in wolf form; humans merely heard grunts or growls.

The other wolf sucked in a breath. "Oh, my dear...he rose to the stars some five summers past. I serve his rightful blooded heir, King Alaric. My mate, Oliver, is his steward."

"This is the second day you have returned. Why do you do so?"

There was a pause, then the elder chuckled. "Oliver thinks I have lost my wits, setting out with horse and cart in this weather. But I am *compelled* to. The order will not leave my mind, as though Leto herself issues it. You must be brought to safety."

Evaine closed her eyes, her whole body shaking with silent sobs. Could it really be true? She would soon be warm? Clean? Fed?

Soon she would be safe?

Swallowing hard, she cleared her throat. "Blanche...I will come. But I may need your help."

"Of course, my dear. Gently, gently."

Slowly, painfully, Evaine shuffled along the narrow den tunnel toward the bramble-covered entrance, trying not to retch as the putrid dirt scraped her fur, and her stiff, weak limbs protested every movement. Yet she still paused a foot from the end, her sire's warning of caution forever in her ears. Was the elder merely pretending? Could there be an entire army of mercenaries just waiting for a foolish princess to leave the den?

A shudder rolled through her body and her belly clenched and twisted in fear. This was it. She was about to place her trust in someone for the first time in two full years.

Leto protect me.

Bracing her paws as best she could, Evaine nudged aside the brambles with her head and launched herself out of the den entrance. The harsh light was blinding, her legs too weak to hold her up, and she collapsed onto the snowy ground at the elder's feet.

"Oh, my dear!" Blanche fussed, leaning down to curve her arms under Evaine's belly and help her rise. "Now, are you able to walk just a few steps to my cart? Then we can... GODDESS."

Evaine froze as she met the elder's shocked gaze. "Is...is something amiss?"

Blanche sank to one knee and bowed her head. "Your Highness! Forgive my overfamiliar speech."

"You know who I am?" whispered Evaine, even now, not quite daring to believe.

"It would take more than grime and frost to disguise the green eyes of a de Wynter. May I ask which daughter of King Hugo and Queen Magdalena you are?"

"Their firstborn. Evaine."

A huge smile wreathed Blanche's face. "Leto's protective and gentle hands have guided us to each other. How blessed am I to be trusted with such an important task. Come, princess. Let us away to the castle. Cook was roasting a side of venison when I left. There'll be spiced lamb and salted pork as well. Nice blazing fire with plenty of cushions to stretch out in front of."

The elder then sank onto all fours so Evaine could use her back as a step to climb onto the sturdy wooden cart. With her trembling limbs and hazy vision, it still felt like ascending a mountain, but eventually she settled onto a clean pile of straw. Blanche dusted the snow from her apron, expertly swung herself up onto the front of the cart, and with a click of the reins they were on their way.

It was a bumpy ride, as the snow hid all manner of rocks and ruts. But after leaving the forest they came upon a well-kept road, and soon they were less than a mile from the imposing visage of Blackstone Castle.

Evaine's jaw dropped. The castle was actually black! Surrounded by snowdrifts and with bright noon light behind it, the massive structure gleamed like ink on parchment and boasted high walls, four soaring towers, and long ramparts with a burly guard every few feet. A wide, deep moat surrounded the castle, and a single gray stone bridge led up to an entrance with huge oak doors and a spiked iron portcullis.

It should have been bleak. Frightening. Yet the strangest sensation of warmth surrounded her as they approached, as though the castle was drawing her close for a loving embrace.

Welcoming her home.

How could she feel such comfort about a place she'd never been before?

"'Tis a fine castle," Evaine whispered.

"Indeed," said Blanche, looking pleased. "Now, not that I'm saying anyone here means you harm, but it might be best if you lie down for a while, Your Highness. Just until we're in the courtyard proper. Then I'll escort you to the Great Hall for all the food you can eat."

"Is...is King Alaric there?" Evaine asked, even saying his name provoking a tingle of anticipation.

"Alas not, princess. He's in London meeting the new human king, Henry Tudor. But he'll be back in a few days at most. Ample time to bathe and feast, yes?"

In human form, her cheeks would be redder than cherries. "Can I eat in the privy chamber?"

Blanche burst out laughing. "I wouldn't make you choose, Your Highness."

For the first time since that fateful day in the Ashcross Castle gardens, a sense of peace washed over Evaine. She drooped wearily, crossing her front paws and dropping her muzzle onto them.

The new king would keep her safe, she was sure of it. He would be gruffly kind like her own sire had been, with silver-touched fur and a weathered countenance. Blanche had neglected to mention Alaric's queen or cubs, but she couldn't wait to meet them all.

Everything would be better now. *Everything.*

———

Eltham Palace

"Now, Sir Alaric, it can be quite overwhelming to meet a king, but you need not be afraid. His Grace is an amiable man, not given to bursts of temper or rash commands. And he is half-Welsh, like yourself! Oh indeed, King Henry will surely look upon you with great favor. Come along, this way, this way. Aren't the tapestries magnificent?"

Alaric clenched his jaw as the young courtier prattled on, seemingly oblivious that Henry Tudor would be the *fourth* human king Alaric had personally sworn fealty to in the past two years. This wasn't even the first occasion at Eltham; both Edward IV and Richard III had held the ceremonies here. Ugh. It was times like this that a wolf king's average life span, around two hundred human years, seemed unendurable. And he couldn't even share his impatience with Ranulf or Darius; they were now cooling their heels in an antechamber as the courtier had insisted each landowner be presented individually.

"Sir Alaric? Are you ready? It is a shame you didn't have time to change your clothing, but I'm sure His Grace won't hold a little travel mud against you. Do ensure you take a knee and bow with all due reverence. We herald a new dawn. The Tudor era shall be far greater than anything gone before!"

Alaric forced himself to nod gravely rather than turn the pompous slug upside down and wash his hair in the nearest chamber pot. Wolves tended to avoid human aristocrats and their gatherings for this reason; even an ice-cold king renowned for diplomacy had his limits.

Soon, a trumpet flourish sounded in the Great Hall, and the large crowd parted to reveal King Henry sitting rather awkwardly on a huge carved oak throne atop the dais at the north end. The human appeared tall but slender, with shoulder-length brown hair and delicate features, and wore black shirt and hose with a beautifully embroidered cream doublet. The heavy chains of state lay around Henry's neck, and a plain gold crown sat atop his head. He was flanked by a small group of favorites including his mother, Lady Margaret; his battlefield savior, Lord Stanley; his uncle, Jasper Tudor; and the Archbishop of Canterbury, John Morton.

The courtier gestured for Alaric to halt, then stepped forward and bowed. "Your Grace, may I present Sir Alaric Dafydd Beaumont of the Welsh Marches, only son of Sir Cyrus Beaumont and Lady Siân Dafydd. A simple and faithful subject come to humbly swear fealty to his sovereign king."

Not by a twitch did Alaric reveal his displeasure at the introduction. Nor did he growl, *You mean you present King Alaric, undisputed ruler of the Western Lands, Alpha Male of the Beaumont gray wolf pack, son and heir of the revered King Cyrus now risen to the stars, and Queen Siân, his beloved mate.*

Diplomacy meant wearing a mask at all times, of never revealing true thoughts or feelings. He couldn't say it was only Hera's spiteful curse that brought him within fifty miles of a human ruler, especially the bloodstained English crown. Alaric's role was to trade in information and strike bargains without raising hackles or suspicions. If anyone knew he was angry, sad, or unsettled, then he'd failed in his duty, and Alaric already had significant obstacles to overcome: he was considerably taller and broader than most humans and would be deemed a threat before he even spoke in his low, growling tone. Even his sire had called him a big lad, while his mother smugly proclaimed him a true Welsh son with shoulders like a mountain range, coalblack hair, and eyes of the purest gold.

Unfortunately, in this hall he could already feel waves of resentment and fear from men gripping their sword hilts. Some discreetly moved closer to the double doors, and Alaric sighed inwardly. Once again, a human royal court needed to believe they faced no more than a gentle giant.

With languid grace, Alaric strolled forward then slowly, deliberately, dropped to one knee. Next, he began the same oath he'd made three times before: "Your Grace. As head of the Beaumont family, I become your liege man of life and limb and truth and earthly honors, bearing to you against all men who love, move, or die, so help me God and the Holy Dame."

Surprisingly, King Henry stood and offered a warm smile. "Arise, Sir Alaric. You are most welcome in my court this Christmastide. I hereby recognize your ancient claim to lands in the Welsh Marches and your authority there. I accept your pledge of fealty. However, unlike previous kings, I do not feel a knighthood adequately honors the service of the Beaumont family in this realm now mine. So it is with good cheer that I confer upon you the title of duke. Henceforth, you shall be known as Duke of Blackstone."

What vicious Hera-spite was this?

Somehow, Alaric managed to quell both his recoil and roar of outrage. Wolves abhorred human titles, and reluctantly accepted only the most minor ones to keep the peace. Every Beaumont before him had been a knight and completely content, because the only title that truly mattered was King of the Western Lands. Now, the tradition had been broken and neither wolf nor human would respect his new status. What had he done to warrant such a travesty?

Alaric cleared his throat, his wolf senses near-drowning in the emotions hurtling toward him like poisoned arrows. Envy from those who had fought at Bosworth Field and been granted far less. Seething fury from the Yorkists who'd watched Alaric pledge to their own side so recently and hated Henry Tudor with every fiber of their being. And contempt from the rest who believed anyone with Welsh blood sat far beneath them. "Your Grace, surely that is too great an honor."

Henry waved a hand. "It is long overdue, *Blackstone*. We

shall meet in the treasury on the morrow before you depart; you'll receive all the documentation and seals for your new title. In return, I'm sure you will offer *generous* tribute to your king."

And there it was, the heart of the matter. Alaric's elevation to duke had nothing to do with his pack's service or Welsh blood, but their goldmines. Henry needed money, and one way to gather it was conferring titles then taxing the new titleholder.

No doubt becoming a duke in the human realm was a very costly exercise.

Alaric gritted his teeth and swept a low bow. At least now he had the measure of the man; Henry was also a diplomat of sorts, hiding a cunning and avaricious soul behind a pleasant smile. Perhaps he would hold the English crown for a while. "As Your Grace wishes."

The human king nodded then turned and whispered to Lady Margaret, *"See? I knew it would work. You fret overmuch, Lady Mother. I shall not be a beggar for long."*

Such impudence! Alaric took several shallow breaths, the urge to change, bare his fangs and claws, and unleash mayhem in the hall nearly overwhelming. That was yet another human flaw: their whispers were a shout to wolf ears. It was time to leave this palace while his sanity remained intact.

Straightening his shoulders, Alaric walked backward ten steps as protocol demanded, then turned and marched to the double doors. All eyes remained upon him, so he forced himself to be cool and calm, to not hurl bodies or tables. But to add insult to injury, the guards inclined their heads and murmured *"Your Grace"* as he passed them.

Needing friendly faces, Alaric continued directly to the antechamber where his brother kings waited.

Darius immediately sprang to his feet. The warrior was perhaps the only wolf in England larger than Alaric, with the scarred countenance and piercing amber gaze of one who embraced war. Human clothing never sat well on Darius, always appearing on the verge of splitting, and his wild brown hair was only partially tamed by a plait secured with a leather strip. Both wolves and humans avoided Darius if possible—he truly looked like Death and Destruction coming to claim them. And he was.

"Well?" growled Darius. "What news? The human king kept you long enough."

Alaric scowled; only in their presence would he ever allow such emotion to show. "Henry conferred a title upon me. I am now a duke."

Ranulf burst out laughing. "Imagine if he actually did. It might start a civil war between wolf and human, just for the insult."

"I'm not jesting," Alaric bit out. "Duke of Blackstone."

Both his brother kings stared at him in shock.

"Henry has a death wish," spat Darius, his lips twisting.

"What exactly did that wretched human say?" said Ranulf, all trace of amusement gone from his too-handsome face.

"That a knighthood did not adequately honor the service of the Beaumont family. Oh yes, and in an entirely unrelated matter, he expects the first generous tribute to be deposited in the treasury tomorrow."

Darius snorted. "So, 'tis you who'll be funding the Tudor court. I wondered who they might rob, for the Plantagenets bled the coffers dry and Henry barely has two pennies to rub together after his campaign. The others ennobled should be damned grateful they won't owe as much, but I wager they aren't."

"No," said Alaric. "They just glared. Mother is going to be furious about this, but at least she'll understand that I couldn't refuse the title. Others won't. Damn Hera-spawned Henry. I wanted to avoid trouble, now he's gone and put a target on my back. It's one thing for wolves and humans to both want Beaumont gold, but must I be dishonored with the rank of *duke*?"

"You have my sympathy, brother," said Ranulf, clapping him on the shoulder. "Thank Leto we were not so blessed, Darius and I would not have borne it with your calm. The only remedy is wine. Let's drain Eltham Palace dry, then hunt all their deer. Oh, and remember it could have been worse: Imagine Guy bloody Saville standing there watching."

Alaric sighed deeply. As Bosworth Field was within the Eastern Lands, the coward Saville had already made his pledge. He rarely set foot outside the border, usually sending mercenaries to do his evil deeds.

In any event, wine would be a good start. Being Duke of Blackstone promised nothing but strife.

TWO

Blackstone Castle

E vaine lay sprawled on a pile of soft velvet cushions in front of a roaring fireplace, her tail flicking lazily as she rested. There might be one square inch of her belly that wasn't stuffed full with roasted venison and the most delicious vegetable pottage she'd ever tasted, but Blanche had left a tray with dried beef strips and a bowl of wine in the event she wished to fill that tiny gap.

Food was all that mattered right now. Not wanting the servants to go to any trouble with a hip bath, Evaine had assured them that a light scrubbing with a bristle brush and warmed bucket of water would be quite sufficient. Even though she was a horribly gaunt and rather tragic collection of fur and bones, as a blooded royal wolf, she was still much larger than most. Attempting to fold her stiff, sore form into a bath would be far too painful, and also offer a frustrating reminder of her continued inability to shift to human form and heal faster.

How she hated feeling so weak!

But she was safe. No, not just safe, cocooned in a well-fortified yet sumptuous castle. Blackstone might look stark and threatening from the outside, but inside it was spotlessly clean with elegant linens, elaborate tapestries, fresh rushes, and an astonishing amount of gold. Plates and goblets, spoons and eating knives, even trays and ladles.

Every female she'd seen had a gold girdle, and their hair was plaited, twisted into a circle, and secured by pretty gold combs. Each male's hose was fastened to their breech belt with a gold buckle, and all their swords had golden hilts. It had made her jaw drop, how casually such a precious and expensive metal was used, but Blanche had explained that the Beaumonts owned many goldmines, far, far more than the humans knew of, and the supply was plentiful. Now Evaine thought about it, King Cyrus and Queen Siân had brought gifts of gold when they'd visited Ashcross Castle. Mother had shaken her head and muttered about spoiled cubs when she'd found her young playfully kicking and batting around palm-sized nuggets.

Yet here at Blackstone, aside from the delicious food, skilled servants, and outrageous amount of gold...there was a specific scent she couldn't stay away from. Somehow it rose above the usual castle smells like meat roasting, wood burning, crushed herbs in the apothecary, beeswax candles, and damp mud from the moat outside. If asked to describe the scent she would sound quite mad, because it was all her favorites blended together: summer rain, green leaves, salt air, fresh lemon, warm leather and a full-bodied red wine. But it didn't matter how often Evaine prowled the castle, she couldn't seem to find the source...although it did seem strongest in the king's library.

To her great shame she had turned a little feral in there, rubbing her head against shelves of leather-bound books, rolling around on a woven rug, and actually curling up on a huge carved oak chair. Leto forgive her, she'd practically licked the soft leather armrests. It was so strange. She knew how to behave like a princess, yet the scent made her feel... wild. Hot and tingly inside.

"Princess? Are you awake?"

Evaine jerked her head up at the elder wolf's words. "Come in, Blanche. I was just woolgathering."

Blanche smiled. "I won't tarry, but Queen Siân has returned from her hunt and wishes to visit. Oh, and we've received word that King Alaric has departed London and will be here by dawn."

"I'm at the queen's command," replied Evaine, gulping. "Whenever she is ready."

"I'll let her know," said Blanche, bobbing a quick curtsy before hurrying away.

Evaine stared at the fire, her belly churning. How would the queen receive her? Siân and Mother had trod warily around each other; while they were similar in temperament, they had very different backgrounds. The Queen of the Western Lands hailed from an ancient line of Welsh aristocratic wolves and met her king at a joust, while Mother had been an outcast and met Father in a tavern. But Siân had suffered greatly; she'd endured a long and difficult travail to birth her only cub. And now she was a widow after the loss of her beloved mate.

Miserably, Evaine examined her ragged gray fur, and only slightly less gaunt frame. In no way did she resemble a princess, the blooded daughter of King Hugo. If only she could change!

"Good afternoon. I trust you are enjoying your stay at Blackstone Castle."

The accent was low and musical, but the words were exceedingly cool. Evaine scrambled inelegantly off the cushions, then turned and knelt on her front legs, a show of submission to Siân Dafydd Beaumont, Queen of the Western Lands. Even in human form the queen was magnificent, tall and plump and beautiful. As wolves abhorred headdresses, her silver-laced black hair was plaited, coiled about her ears, and covered with a sheer gold veil. But her golden eyes glowed with fierce intelligence, her creamy skin boasted few lines, and although she wore a simple blue velvet gown with slashed sleeves and square neckline, Queen Siân *looked* noble.

"I thank you, Queen Siân of the Western Lands, for your generous hospitality. Please forgive my current state, I am unable to change at present—"

"You claim to be Princess Evaine of the Eastern Lands," said the queen sharply as she moved closer and gripped Evaine's muzzle. "Others might be fooled by a tale of woe in winter, but not I. There shall be no more imposters in this royal court. Look at me."

Slowly, Evaine raised her head and met the older wolf's steely gaze.

Queen Siân sucked in a harsh breath. "A familiar green, but I'll hear more proof. Tell me something only a de Wynter would know."

This was the occasion to ignore her sire's counsel and be bold. Her very future depended on it. "Mother and Father sent me away with two ladies and two warriors

35

before Guy Saville attacked Ashcross Castle. I've been in hiding for ten long years, the last two entirely alone, and I don't know where my sisters and brother are. I miss them more than words can describe. As for something only a de Wynter would know...the last time I saw you and King Cyrus, he gifted us cubs with a black velvet sack of large gold nuggets, twice the size of our paws, to play with."

The silence was so prolonged that the crackle and hiss of the fire sounded louder than a gunpowder explosion. Then the hand gripping Evaine's muzzle slid further up to gently scratch behind her ears, the motherly touch unleashing a broken howl from the very depths of Evaine's soul.

"Come here, sweet one," said Queen Siân softly, sinking onto the pile of cushions and holding out her arms.

Evaine was far too big to curl up on the other wolf's lap, but that didn't stop her trying; she nearly knocked the queen over in her yearning to be petted and soothed like a cub. "I lost everyone I loved," she choked out.

"I know," said the queen, as she stroked Evaine's fur and began carefully removing the stubborn burrs. "Such loss is an unendurable pain that does not lessen with time, no matter what the poets say. But you must get up when knocked down, or that monster Guy Saville wins. You are alive, Evaine, and that is a most wondrous victory, a ray of light in the darkness. I know Alaric, my son and king, will proclaim that as long as the usurper holds the Book of Lore and the Eastern throne, you may remain as our most honored guest. If it pleases you, of course."

"It does," sniffled Evaine, shamelessly bunting the queen's hand for more ear-scratching. Being starved of food was one thing, but in many ways, being starved of touch and affection was equally terrible. Now was not the time for a full-grown wolf's pride. "I adore Blackstone Castle. I swear it welcomed me when I arrived. Everything is lovely and it smells so divine."

Queen Siân laughed. "You mean the kitchens? I will confess I am easily lured from my bed by the aroma of freshly prepared meat—our cook has a skilled hand."

"No, the other scent. I get faint wafts of it everywhere, in the Great Hall and the solar and the shrine to Leto and her divine twins. However, I cannot find the source. It is strongest in the king's library and I just want to roll around in it all the time...oh, forgive me, that was crass," finished Evaine awkwardly, as the other wolf's hand actually stilled.

"Is it one scent, like a flower?" asked the queen quietly. "Or perhaps many scents together, all of them pleasing?"

Evaine turned her head, her eyes widening. "Many. How did you know that? I thought I was losing my wits."

The strangest expression crossed Queen Siân's face, as though she felt great joy and great pain at the same time. But how could that be? And why would such emotions be provoked over talk of a mystery scent?

"You are not losing your wits, my dear," said the queen eventually. "But we shall see how the ribbon unfolds. In the meantime, you need to rest. And eat. The sooner you are stronger, the sooner you'll be able to change. I shall join you here for supper later, and we can talk some more."

"Of course," said Evaine eagerly.

After one more affectionate head scratch, the queen departed, and Evaine settled once again in front of the fire. It was disconcerting how swiftly she'd felt at home here, although...

Evaine glanced longingly in the direction of the library.

NICOLA DAVIDSON

Would one more visit really be so bad?

———

"Nearly home, Your G...er...my king."

Alaric glanced sideways at Wesley as they loped along the snow-covered countryside, entirely unamused at the gleeful twinkle in his squire's eyes. The wolfling always behaved when they were beyond pack lands. However, the closer they were to Blackstone Castle and his mother Blanche's fierce protection, the bolder he became. But right now, when Alaric was freezing his balls off in the frigid dawn air and his stomach still churned from lackluster fare at the two human inns they'd stopped at, he was in no mood for jests about his wretched "gift" from Henry. "Blackstone is still several miles away, boyo. Far enough that your mother couldn't save you if you fell down a well."

Wesley huffed out a breath. "Diplomats never say what they mean. King Darius would simply lift me by the throat and growl *I'm going to kill you*. But you very nicely, very calmly, utter things like 'if you fell down a well'. Doesn't it ever get weary, playing word games?"

Yes.

In human form, Alaric might have sighed and rubbed the bridge of his nose for it was too damned cold and too damned early for such a probing question. Wesley did that sometimes, amongst his mischievous antics and undoubted squire skills: asked a question that was startlingly insightful. One day he might well be an excellent advisor.

Today was definitely not that day.

Besides, even on his own lands and with excellent wolf

vision, Alaric didn't like to linger outside in this unholy brew of fresh snow, blustery wind, and pitch-black darkness. It was the kind of weather only mercenaries and brigands enjoyed, not to mention that his guards, carts and luggage, and horses were far behind them. Usually, he and Wesley remained with the procession, especially when transporting important documents or gifts. But for some unknown reason, his senses were urging him to return to the castle with all haste.

Was there a threat nearby? Had his mother been injured during her planned hunt?

Anything was possible with so many mercenaries lurking. Although Alaric ruthlessly crushed the violent packs whenever they emerged, there were always more. Also, the risk would only grow now the bounty on the de Wynter heirs had increased again, and he'd been made a bloody duke by the human king. Wolves would deem that a weakness to be exploited.

"Forget word games, think only on being a squire, wolfling," growled Alaric eventually. "Perhaps one day you'll master that."

"Come now," said Wesley, his pale eyes glinting in the darkness. "Even the great King of the Western Lands could admit I am most adequate. Praise me. I dare you."

In truth, he *was* most adequate.

The wolfling might try Alaric's patience daily, but Wesley had become rather accomplished with bow and arrow, had a skilled touch with horses, and took great care with Alaric's belongings. As a young wolf, he was also much smaller and leaner, so created no spectacle in a human crowd—a rather useful information-gathering tool within palaces. It would be a sad day indeed when Wesley fully matured and ventured away to find his mate, for the wolfling provided a great deal of mood-easing entertainment at Blackstone Castle. Much as Alaric loved and respected his mother the elder queen, they did quarrel on occasion. She had never accepted Theda, actually daring to claim his mate was an imposter who had *etched* a mark on her neck and his wrist.

Alaric cursed under his breath. No. Theda had been his mate, she had passed without experiencing a breeding heat, and now he would be alone until his own death. He just had to accept that fact. As did his mother.

"I don't puff smoke on demand," he replied. "If you receive praise from me, you'll have earned it. Besides, Blanche commends you enough for everyone."

Wesley groaned theatrically then threw himself onto a mound of snow, rolled onto his back and twitched his tail in the air. "Mother praise and king praise are two very different things. If you refuse, I shall hurl myself down, hmmm, at least two feet. Do you truly want no injury whatsoever weighing heavily on your soul?"

Somehow, Alaric quelled both his irritation and reluctant amusement. Was this what it felt like to be a father? A constant inner war of pride and exasperation as they were provoked by wolflings? "Very well. At the Eltham armory, Henry complimented me on my sword and horse. Said I must have a competent squire."

Wesley sprang up, shook the snow from his fur and preened before marching once more. "I would tell Henry he seems adequate for a human king, even if his line is completely unexceptional. I mean he's hardly following an ancient line of legends...like the Beaumonts."

Alaric's lips twitched. "Perhaps you'll succeed as a

courtier after all. But first you must master the skill of silence."

"Yes, my king. From now until we reach the castle, not a single word shall pass my lips. Even if you beg me to speak. Even if I fall down a well. Nothing. I am mute."

Leto, give me strength.

However, as Blackstone Castle's imposing towers finally came into view, Alaric found himself bounding down the road, so swiftly that Wesley made a low whine of protest as he struggled to keep up.

When Alaric approached the drawbridge, he paused and howled, a long, low guttural sound to let all and sundry know their king had returned. Moments later, guards with torches appeared, and the sound of clinking chains echoed in the chilly air as the portcullis was raised.

Once inside the safety of the castle courtyard, he and Wesley entered a small gatehouse filled with a variety of warm clothing and changed into human form. These days Alaric rarely even considered the process; for him it happened quickly and relatively painlessly, a brief stretching and crunching as his limbs elongated, his fangs became teeth, claws became fingers and toes, fur became a dusting of body hair, and his tail disappeared. Poor Wesley took much longer; it could be rather miserable for wolflings, but still better than a cub's first change, which was pure agony. However, no matter how old or experienced the wolf, every change resulted in a naked human form, hence the clothing to wear.

"Ready?" asked Alaric, now fully dressed in linen shirt, woolen hose, and fur-lined doublet.

"Ready," said Wesley, nodding as he hastily fastened his hose.

Surprisingly, Alaric's mother waited outside the gatehouse. While he was relieved to see her hale and hearty, it was highly unusual for her to greet him at such an early hour. Queen Siân loathed mornings.

"My son and king," she said, curtsying deeply.

"Lady Mother," Alaric replied carefully. "Is something amiss?"

The elder queen pulled her fur-lined robe closer. "Perhaps we could move to the privacy of your library?"

"You don't wish to sup in the Great Hall?"

"No. It must be your library."

Alaric frowned, every instinct near-bellowing a warning. But after dismissing Wesley to Blanche's care, Alaric followed his mother across the courtyard and into the castle proper. As soon as he stepped through the huge double doors, a faint scent wafted around him.

A new *delicious* scent. Like wildflowers and fresh herbs and sunshine.

"Did Blanche source new rushes?" he asked. "Or a different candle recipe, perhaps? I like it."

His mother made an odd sound that almost seemed like...laughter? "Hurry, my son. The library," she repeated, gathering her robe hem and near-running up the spiral steps to the second floor.

Utterly baffled at her behavior, Alaric continued to his favorite room in the castle, the one he spent most of his time and had furnished accordingly. Yet the moment he stepped into the library, he froze as the scent from below hit him like an anvil, overwhelming his senses, and wrapping around him like a cloak.

Goddess.

He sucked in a breath, his entire body craving it like a parched wolf craves water. The heady aroma was everywhere, yet how could that be? The room was empty. And he couldn't even describe it, for what had seemed so innocently pleasing downstairs had a far different element up here. Something raw and carnal, like the hottest, wettest cunt, begging to be filled.

In the blink of an eye, his cock was harder than stone.

What is this madness? Have I been poisoned? Enchanted?

"Alaric? Are you well?"

Embarrassment scorched across his cheekbones, and he stumbled across the room to sit behind his desk and hide his affliction. Then he groaned softly.

Goddess.

How could it be even stronger here? Soon he'd be grinding himself against his damned desk!

"Quite well," he bit out, his fists clenching as his cock ached and he fought the urge to rip off his hose and spend all over his chair. The scent made him want to rut until he couldn't move. It *urged* him to.

"You don't *look* well, my son," chirped his mother gaily.

Why is she so damned cheerful? Has she lost her wits?

"If you have something to say, Mother, then by all means say it," Alaric growled.

The elder queen drew herself up to her full height and inclined her head. "Very well. While you were in London with the human king, Blanche rescued a gaunt, starving waif who was hiding in an abandoned fox's den. In a great turn of fortune's wheel, that waif is...Princess Evaine de Wynter."

His jaw dropped. Then the warmth of pure relief kindled inside him, flowing everywhere like molten gold. "Are you sure?"

"I'm absolutely certain."

Alaric couldn't help smiling at something so momentous. A de Wynter heir, alive! "I could not be more pleased. That is glorious news."

"Oh, that is only half the tale, my son. The other half is even more important."

"What could possibly be more noteworthy than Princess Evaine, safe in my castle?"

"She is your fated mate."

———

How had she not known that Blackstone Castle was enchanted?

Evaine padded back and forth across her chamber, blinking wearily, her body craving sleep but her mind racing faster than a hungry wolf chasing a deer.

That howl.

Until the day she rose to the stars, she would never forget the low, guttural, *powerful* sound. It had jolted her awake, and she'd scrambled up off the cushions so fast her paws skidded on the cold stone surface as she made for the door, her throat actually hurting as she tried to howl a reply and only coughed and spluttered. Until her mind caught up to her instincts and asked a most pertinent question: *what are you doing?*

Since then, Evaine had swung between pacing and staring out the chamber window as new guards took their posts along the ramparts and around the gatehouse, and various castle servants began their daily tasks of preparing food, tending animals, doing laundry, and hammering weapons in the armory.

A princess waiting. Watching.

Who am I waiting and watching for?

Evaine shook her whole body, trying to clear the

44

lethargy, the fogginess of her thoughts. Several times the previous day she'd tried to change to human form, but no matter how much she urged herself on, shutting her eyes and imagining arms and legs and long fair hair...nothing. Queen Siân had tried to comfort her, counseling that time and rest and food would resolve the issue, but Evaine wanted to change *now*.

A brief knock at the door made her tail twitch, then Blanche bustled in carrying a bucket of steaming water, a cloth, and a large platter of thickly sliced pork.

Evaine's mouth watered. "Good morning, Blanche."

The elder wolf beamed. "Good morning! Forgive me for being a little late—my youngest cub Wesley returned in the early hours and had many tales to tell about Eltham Palace. Naturally, I had to prepare his favorite breakfast. Cook never puts enough pork slices on a platter, wolflings can't survive on a quarter loin! Especially not a wolfling who is the *king's squire*."

"Was it, er, Wesley who howled?" Evaine asked, her heart beginning to pound.

Blanche chortled. "Ha! My sweet babe would adore above all things to have a howl so low and strong and constant. Alas, his range hits much higher notes. No, the howl you heard was King Alaric, who is finally home from London. And he wishes to meet you! So eat your breakfast, then I'll give your fur a nice, gentle scrub."

An audience with the King of the Western Lands!

For a brief moment, Evaine forgot decorum and her shoulders dipped in despair. Usually, all formal occasions took place in human form, as it was an opportunity for great pomp and ceremony. They would sit at long trestle tables near-groaning with food, drink wine from silver goblets, and wear magnificent clothes and jewels to demonstrate the ruling pack's wealth and power. How a royal bestowed and received hospitality was a matter of fierce pride and even fiercer judgment; bad enough she'd met the elder queen as a wolf, but to greet the king like this would be a mark of shame on the de Wynter name.

"Right now?" she asked softly.

Blanche's gaze turned sympathetic. "I know it's not ideal, Your Highness, but King Alaric insisted. He'll not be offended in any way; Queen Siân explained the situation. My master is eager to make the acquaintance of King Hugo's daughter—your sire and his were such great friends. It's a shame you are not acquainted already, but then-Prince Alaric was beginning his knightly training when his parents visited the Eastern Lands."

Evaine glared at the floor, her claws extending and retracting several times as she fought an inner war. Half of her yearned to meet the owner of that most glorious alpha howl with all haste. The other half wanted to wait until she could stroll on two legs into his presence and gracefully curtsy, wearing an elegant gown with a long train, gems winking on her fingers, and her neatly plaited blond hair shimmering under the warm glow of beeswax candles.

Eventually, she sighed. "Very well."

Far too soon for her peace of mind, Evaine finished the pork, succumbed to Blanche's careful yet brisk sponge bath, and was making her way to the king's library. Thankfully, he had courteously left the door ajar so she didn't have to demean herself further and scratch at it to be let in.

She almost paused and declared herself. Instead, Evaine moaned as she was struck by a wave of the delectable library scent, a scent that seemed to pull her inside, and she charged into the room.

Goddess.

46

Whatever she'd been expecting of King Alaric, it certainly wasn't the most gloriously handsome male she'd ever seen in her life. He wasn't an elder wolf at all...and he was *huge*. Much taller and broader than her own sire, and rather than fair hair, this king's shoulder-length locks were as black as his castle. She'd heard chatter of the king's Spanish grandmother, and the warm, sun-kissed hue of his skin certainly offered proof of that. But most startling of all, under stern black brows, his eyes were pure gold.

That gaze was like being seared by the sun.

Without warning, the back of her neck began to tingle, and Evaine whimpered in confusion as heat coursed through her veins. Then she cried out in pain as her wolf form twisted and cracked and lengthened, making her writhe as she changed.

Oh no. Oh no. Oh no.

As she lay naked on a rug wincing at the cramping and stiffness of her human limbs, the king growled, a rough, raw sound that caressed her flesh. Abruptly all discomfort was forgotten, and Evaine gasped as her nipples hardened to jewel-like points and a shocking wetness gathered between her legs.

What on earth was happening?

Her mind, still so enmeshed in human customs, bellowed that she was behaving like a harlot and should cover herself or turn onto her side and curl into a ball. But her body refused, reveling in the way the king stared at her with such blatant hunger. Such need. When Father had gazed at Mother like that, they kissed. Sometimes they'd dashed away saying they were late for an important meeting.

Does King Alaric wish to kiss me?

The unruly thought made Evaine burn, and she pressed

her thighs together to try and ease the ache. Why wasn't the king doing something? Why wasn't he making it stop?

"P-please," Evaine choked out. "Help me."

King Alaric closed his eyes briefly, then strode forward, his big hands tearing at the buttons fastening his doublet. After shaking the garment out, he draped it around her shoulders, cocooning her in fur-lined warmth and his heady scent. "Here."

With a happy sigh, Evaine pulled it closer around her, rubbing her cheek against the soft collar. The doublet was far too big, reaching below her knees, but it was so comforting to wear that she might never take it off. "It's lovely. Thank you."

"Your hair is caught, princess. Do not move," he growled, before deftly freeing a heavy lock snagged on the embroidery just under the collar.

But as his fingers grazed her shoulder, Evaine gasped at the jolt of sensation.

Yes. Touch me. Touch me everywhere.

"Your Grace," she said beseechingly, moving restlessly up onto her knees.

He flinched. "Don't call me that."

Evaine's brow furrowed. "Your Grace" was how a dignitary correctly addressed the ruler of another kingdom; it was only "My King" or "My Queen" in their own realm. "Forgive me. What do you prefer? Sire? Master?"

His golden eyes glittered, and that strange ache between her legs became an unbearable pulsing throb. Goddess, she wanted to touch herself. Lie on her soft cushions in front of the fireplace and just stroke that wet, sensitive place until...

Until what?

King Alaric rubbed his bearded jaw, then marched over

to the library window and rested his hands on the stone wall before pressing his forehead to the glass, putting at least ten feet between them. Unaccountably, the sudden distance felt like a physical blow, and a soft whine of unhappiness escaped her throat before she could halt it.

"Damn it," he snarled, slapping his palm against the stone. "She's wrong. My mother is *wrong*. 'Tis no more than wishful thinking. Perhaps you don't know this, princess, but I was mated. Queen Theda died in a fall last summer. She tripped on her gown hem, tumbled awkwardly down some stairs, and broke her neck. I was *mated*. Do you understand? My chance at love and passion, at being happy, at fathering cubs is *gone*."

Evaine could only stare. While she knew the information to be true—Blanche had mentioned the late queen—every part of her rejected it. "I mourn your loss."

"Do not pity me," said the king grimly. "I failed to keep my mate safe. To keep her content in my bed. Far worse, I was unbroken by her passing. So if you think I am some sort of noble hero, you are very much mistaken. I will remain a lone wolf, as Leto decrees, for being naught but ice."

"*Ice*?" The incredulous word burst from her lips, far beyond the realm of caution or courtesy. "How can you think you are ice, Alaric, when all I see in your eyes is fire?"

Oh no.

Evaine groaned inwardly. For the first time in many, many years, she had allowed her boldness free rein, and instead of following protocol, she had called the King of the Western Lands by his given name. And said something highly inappropriate.

"Forgive me," she said contritely. "I spoke out of turn."

Oddly, the king did not turn to face her. "Go now."

"But—"

"*Leave.*"

Every instinct she possessed insisted the command be ignored. Yet clearly she'd tried the king's patience enough this day, so Evaine hastily bobbed a curtsy, gathered his doublet tightly around her body, and hurried from the library.

She would make this right. Somehow.

CHAPTER
THREE

How can you think you are ice, Alaric, when all I see in your eyes is fire?

For the entire day, Princess Evaine's words had spun around in his mind. Well, that and a scene that would remain permanently lodged there: her lying naked before him.

Alaric's fists clenched as he stood in front of his bedchamber looking glass, Wesley brushing the back of his gold-embroidered cream doublet, to ensure it was spotless for tonight's banquet.

Evaine was the most beautiful woman in creation. Fair hair like sunshine, creamy skin, huge green eyes with thick black lashes, and rosy lips begging to be kissed. It had physically hurt to see her too-slender frame, to know she'd been forced to hide and starve just to live. But that hadn't halted a fierce wave of lust; his mouth had watered to taste those jutting pink nipples, to part the blond bush between her thighs and feast until she'd screamed herself hoarse and drenched his tongue in sweet cunt honey. Draping his doublet around her so she wouldn't be cold had been as natural as breathing. Really, Evaine should only wear clothing provided by him, although he'd known a moment of pure alarm that his doublet might be unworthy. Nothing but the finest of silks and velvets, the costliest of jewels, the softest, most supple leather shoes could adorn such loveliness.

Stop. Evaine is not for you. Theda was your fated mate and she is dead. This scent you smell, the raging lust...it's just your mind playing tricks after staying at the human court and will soon be gone.

Alaric took several deep breaths, relieved to have a completely logical reason for his unsettled temperament. Of course he would be on edge! Bloody Henry had foisted a dukedom upon him, collected a pile of gold for the "gift", and made him a future target for both wolf and human. Besides, it was deep winter. All wolves ran a little mad in winter, especially with breeding season approaching. While only some mated females went into a week-long breeding heat, it affected the whole castle as everyone absorbed the insatiable need in the air. Between January and March, Alaric readily forgave the antics of mated pairs in his pack; the constant, frenzied rutting, the need for copious food and drink, the way even his most sensible, decorous male courtiers sported foolish grins and stumble-walked because their cocks hurt from overuse. They truly couldn't help themselves.

Indeed, these strange feelings weren't his own, but excitement and anticipation from the mated wolves around him. While they unleashed their desires, he needed to behave like a king, cool and calm and composed.

"Are you content with the fit, my king?" asked Wesley as he stepped back. "I can fetch the tailor if need be."

Alaric peered hard at the looking glass, examining all

angles and checking every seam, button, and fastening. However, he found no flaw with his white linen shirt, black woolen hose, the embroidered cream doublet, or the gold circlet he usually wore atop his head. Even his hair sat neatly on his shoulders for once, and his calf-length leather boots were polished to a shine. He *looked* like a king.

Perhaps now he was back at Blackstone surrounded by his own pack rather than humans, he would feel like a king again and be able to provide the generous hospitality that Princess Evaine rightly expected.

"No, you've done well," Alaric said gruffly.

Wesley beamed. "We must have you looking just so for the princess!"

Alaric's head jerked around. "Beg pardon?"

His squire gulped. "Er...well, any king must appear to best advantage when entertaining another royal, yes?"

"Yes," agreed Alaric reluctantly, inwardly frowning at his own sharp reaction. He was an experienced diplomat, not a hot-headed fool. "Come, we must escort the ladies into the Great Hall."

Soon, he and Wesley waited outside the double doors for the elder queen and Princess Evaine. When the two women descended the stairs, Alaric's breath caught at the glorious sight of his guest, who wore an emerald-green gown with a gold underskirt and gold sleeves. Evaine's blond hair was confined in a long plait that bounced gently against her back, and the square bodice of her gown framed a heavy gold necklace set with diamonds, a piece from the Beaumont vault.

My jewels. Right where they belong.

His mother approached and curtsied deeply, elegant as always in a gown of rich amethyst studded with pearls over a silver underskirt, her dark hair plaited and coiled at her neck, and covered with a sheer veil. "My son and king. Doesn't Evaine look beautiful? I had my ladies adjust a gown, and thought something from the vault would set it off nicely."

Alaric nodded brusquely as Evaine curtsied and her gown bodice strained against the curves of her breasts. "Indeed, Lady Mother. Shall we proceed into the banquet?"

"Yes!" Siân replied, smiling. "Wesley, dear boy, would you escort your queen to the dais?"

"Be my great honor," said Wesley, his cheeks flushed red as he offered his arm.

Annoyed at how easily his mother had out-maneuvered him, Alaric reluctantly held out his own arm. "Princess?"

"Thank you," Evaine said softly, curling her hand around it.

Even through a few layers of clothing, he felt her touch like a brand.

Alaric cursed under his breath as his cock began throbbing.

Calm. Cool. Composed. Remember, none of these feelings are real.

He gestured to the guards, who bowed and opened the doors to the Great Hall. A loud trumpet fanfare from the gallery soared to the high-beamed roof, then the massive crowd parted to allow the four of them a clear path to the raised dais at the north end of the hall. All eyes were upon them, yet most seemed to be gazing at Evaine with fond smiles, as happy as he'd been to know a de Wynter heir was alive and the murderer Guy Saville hadn't won a total victory.

Yet before he could seat Evaine at the far end of the table, his mother took the chair, smiling sweetly as she did so. Now only two places remained, his chair in the middle, and the chair to his left...where the queen always sat.

"Princess," Alaric said curtly as he pulled the left chair out for her, now acutely aware that the collective pack gaze had turned first shocked then speculative. Queen Siân had held that seat for over one hundred and eighty years, first as queen, then as elder queen—only Theda had temporarily displaced her. For her to concede it once again so publicly and cheerfully...

He turned and glared at his mother. "We shall speak later."

"As you wish," she replied, inclining her head, utterly unrepentant.

Alaric clenched his jaw, but turned to his pack and began a brief speech, informing them of Henry's dukedom gift—which caused prolonged and very loud outrage in the hall—and that Princess Evaine would remain as an honored guest at Blackstone indefinitely, but for her protection, and that of the pack, the news must remain within the castle walls for now.

Once he'd finished, Alaric rang a gold bell and the hall became a hive of activity as servants rushed to set up trestle tables and long wooden benches for everyone attending the feast. All those on guard duty, or with important tasks away from the Great Hall, had already received their supper; no one under Beaumont protection ever went hungry, not here in the castle, nor anywhere on his lands.

About a quarter hour later, two large spun sugar sculptures were carried out, one of the Beaumont coat of arms, and another of the de Wynters...which were then placed side by side in front of him on the high table.

Alaric groaned inwardly. Was every bloody soul he

knew matching him with Evaine? This was far beyond the realm of mere courtesy.

Impatiently, he beckoned the procession of food to begin, and countless servants moved into the hall with platters of beef, pork, venison, chicken, stuffed goose, an array of vegetables, pasties and pies, salted fish, and honey cakes. Wolves preferred savory dishes; the kitchens rarely served tarts, comfits or sweetmeats like the humans enjoyed, but no one could resist a honey cake. As per protocol, the procession halted first in front of the high table so they could make their selections.

Alaric gestured for Evaine to be served, and after licking her lips in a way that made his toes curl, she chose beef, venison, a serving of vegetables and several honey cakes. A servant nodded politely, then began skillfully cutting neat slices of meat.

Fury blasted through Alaric. Evaine wasn't being served the juiciest, rarest, most tender parts!

"What are you doing?" Alaric bit out.

The servant looked at him in confusion. "Beg pardon, my king, I'm carving Her Highness's preferences."

"But not the best!" Alaric snarled. "Anyone who dares to serve Princess Evaine less than the very finest food and wine on the best gold dishes...the freshest herbed water to wash her hands and the crispest linen napkin for her shoulder...will not survive the night!"

Absolute silence reigned in the Great Hall. In truth it was astonishing how quiet five hundred hungry wolves could be, but not a foot or finger tapped, not a spoon dipped or eating dagger sliced as pack members stared at him, their eyes wide and mouths agape. They were stunned at their king's unprecedented show of temper, but not nearly as stunned as he was.

His mother cleared her throat, but her eyes positively *twinkled*. "Now that you understand the importance, do carve as your king has instructed."

The fright cleared from the servant's face and he bowed, abruptly appearing almost...*jaunty*? "Forgive the misstep, my king. I did not know, but now I do. We all do. Of course I will carve the choicest slices for Her Highness. It is my honor."

Alaric scowled. Everyone in the whole damned castle, including him, had run mad.

The sooner this banquet was over, the better.

———

She was eating the most delicious food imaginable, her wine goblet and plate were made of gold, and the most handsome, best-scented king in the entire realm had growled at a servant for not giving her the finest cuts of meat. Was this real? Or would she soon wake up and discover herself still starving and freezing in an abandoned fox den?

Evaine swallowed the last bite of honey cake and sat back in her chair, her stomach pleasantly full. Banquets were truly magnificent, and hopefully no one here had guessed that this was her first time attending one, let alone as a guest of honor. Mother and Father had often hosted banquets and tourneys at Ashcross Castle, but their cubs were only permitted to attend events during the day, as they became too loud and mischievous at night. She, Isabel, Cecily, and Lucan had pleaded to no avail to join in the dancing and feasting. Fortunately the musicians grinned and pretended naught was amiss when four furry cherubs belly-crawled into the gallery overlooking the Great Hall and peeped down at the festivities.

Isabel had admired the pageantry and processions of food, especially the elaborately dressed goose or boar's head. Cecily hoped to hear conversations from emissaries in French and Gaelic and Latin, so she could attempt to translate a few words. Lucan loved the various weapons on display: the decorative sword sheaths, the deadly pikes held by the guards, the jeweled eating daggers, and his tail would twitch this way and that, as though engaged in a duel. But Evaine enjoyed the music most, the way the notes soared and danced in the air, how everyone laughed and clapped and stomped their feet to the steady beat of the drum, the lilting flute or the rich harp. Music was like food for the soul, but also an excellent way to be close to the one you loved. When Mother and Father had danced, they gazed into each other's eyes like the rest of the world ceased to exist.

"Princess?"

King Alaric's gruff voice in her ear sent a sensual shiver through Evaine and made the back of her neck tingle. It was the strangest sensation; sometimes it felt like a little insect crawling on her nape, but when she reached up to swat it away, there was nothing there.

"Er, yes?" Evaine replied, offering a quick smile.

"Is aught amiss? You appear a little saddened."

Dismay crashed through her. If the Beaumont pack thought her haughty or ungrateful, she would not be welcome at Blackstone very long. A lie reached the tip of Evaine's tongue...then halted as she stared into the king's fathomless gold eyes.

I cannot actually lie to him!

Evaine blinked. "I was just remembering," she blurted.

"When we were cubs, my brother and sisters and I would hide in the gallery with the musicians and watch the feasting and dancing below. I loved listening to the harp and flute and drums. Music makes me happy."

"Do you wish to dance?" asked King Alaric. "I can have the hall cleared at once."

"No," she said swiftly. "I...er..."

Once more, his golden gaze compelled the truth.

"I cannot," Evaine whispered painfully, her cheeks flushing red. "I do not know how. At Ashcross Castle, all wolflings were given lessons, but we were too young when we fled."

"I understand," he replied, his hand hovering above hers as if he meant to pat it. "My squire, Wesley, is currently trying to learn. It has reached the point where no she-wolf will partner him, not even Blanche, for he simply cannot stay in time to music and crushes toes like a falling anvil. If a pack warrior is ill-disciplined, their punishment is an hour tutoring Wesley. Nothing could be harsher; he also likes to talk. A lot."

A giggle bubbled within and escaped before she could swallow it down. "Oh dear. Perhaps if your warriors are so well-versed in toe torture, you might spare one to instruct me?"

"No," the king growled, his eyes flashing dangerously. "I will teach you. Everything."

Evaine bit her lip, inhaling unsteadily as the now-familiar throb began between her thighs. Each day it seemed to grow fiercer, heating her from the inside. Now that she'd moved from the fireside cushions to a feather bed, she kicked away her sheets and quilt at night so the cold winter air might ease her feverish flesh. Last evening had been the worst so far; she'd slid her hand down between her legs and touched the crisp hair, the delicate petals and tender, swollen bud there. But the resulting jolt of sensation had been too overwhelming and she'd ceased at once.

She whimpered. "I...I..."

"Evaine," he said harshly, his gaze aimed directly at her lap. "No."

Mortification scorched across her cheekbones. Goddess, she was actually pressing the heel of her hand to her mound! At the high table. At a *banquet*. Her only saving grace: the rest of the pack were unaware due to the heavy linen tablecloth that draped over the front to the dais floor.

But the king had seen her touch herself.

"Forgive me," Evaine whispered, deliberately placing her hands on the table. "I seem to have forgotten all proper graces since I arrived here. Are you overwarm? I feel flushed. Perhaps I need some air. You have four fireplaces in this hall—it is certainly not cold!"

Even hearing her own prattle, words she simply could not halt herself from saying, was embarrassing. Why couldn't she behave like a normal she-wolf around him? Be witty and graceful and elegant like Queen Siân?

As though the other female heard her silent cry, the queen abruptly rose from her chair and walked around the back of the table toward her. "Evaine, will you stroll with me? I would adore to show you the tapestries on the far wall."

"Yes!" said Evaine, nearly knocking over her chair in her haste to stand. "A stroll. Yes. Will you excuse me, King Alaric?"

The king's jaw visibly clenched like he might refuse, yet a moment later, his face smoothed and cleared into a diplomat's mask. "Of course, princess. My Lady Mother is a skilled embroiderer and her great talent is evidenced all over the castle. Go on, there are other conversations I must have."

Both Evaine and Queen Siân curtsied, then ambled from the dais toward a row of large and intricately embroidered tapestries decorating the entire west wall. While many of the pack were still eating, a few tables had already been cleared and put away in anticipation of the dancing to come.

"You know," said the queen, as she linked her arm with Evaine's, "After I met King Cyrus at the joust, may Leto bless his star-soul, I stalked him *relentlessly*. Or perhaps we stalked each other, for we kept meeting. I think I waited, hmmm, two days before I succumbed to my carnal urges and pounced on him. In a *stable*. Do you know how long it takes to remove straw from clothing?"

Evaine almost tripped on her gown at the startlingly frank admission. "Er...I...ah...no?"

Queen Siân laughed merrily. "A very long time. I certainly hope you make a far better location choice when you pounce."

Goddess. Her cheeks might actually warm the entire castle now. "When I...*pounce*?" Evaine mumbled, as though she'd not considered kissing King Alaric about one thousand times.

The queen's amusement faded. She gently guided Evaine closer to the wall so they wouldn't be overheard. "Oh, my poor dear, I fear you have spent far too long alone or observing the ways of humans rather than our own. While we have a human form, we are *not* human and do not follow their priest-led beliefs about piety, chastity and modesty. Wolves are carnal creatures and sating lust with a consenting partner is entirely natural. This is especially true when we find our fated mate and crave release anytime, anywhere, in all ways possible. Otherwise...we *will* run mad."

"But how do you know when you've found your fated mate?" asked Evaine, her heart aching. Such conversations were usually held between parent and wolfling, and right now she missed her mother and father more than ever. Although she greatly liked and admired the elder queen, it was rather awkward asking the mother of the male she wished to pounce on...about pouncing.

Queen Siân nodded thoughtfully. "I think you know in your soul, but your body offers clues. Firstly, that delectable scent you want to roll in; no one else can smell your mate's particular blend. Your neck tingling is another...when they pleasure you, the mark will fully appear and cannot be removed. When you are intimate and they bite that mark as you each spend, it unlocks your bonded mind link. Here, look at my neck."

The elder queen lifted her hair, and Evaine studied the pristine, celestial-blue grouping of two stars with a crown above it. Just as beautiful as Mother's had been.

Evaine then glanced back at the huge crowd of wolves around them. How many were bonded mates? Were there any still searching? Wait. Had that male just kissed the male next to him on the cheek?

She turned back to the queen. "Er..."

"Just ask, my dear. The only bad question is the one that remains in your head."

"Are all mates a male and female pair? Or can it be something else?"

Queen Siân smiled. "Oh no, every pack has pairs of males and pairs of females. When matching hearts and souls, Leto cares not for the body they are in. Have you met

Bardolf, my son's captain of the guard, and Willie, the castle marshal? They are bonded mates, and foster two cubs who lost their birth parents in battle. You'll not see a more loving family."

I want my own family. To be Alaric's bonded mate and mother of his cubs.

The thought crashed into Evaine's mind, so unexpected yet so powerful, that she actually gasped. The back of her neck burned, and she turned her head to see the king looking at her, his gaze intense.

Evaine bit her lip. He was simply too far away. This would not do. "Queen Siân, would you excuse me?"

The older wolf grinned. "Of course. Go and pounce. Just remember, straw is bad, beds and desks are good."

————

Was he actually losing his wits?

Alaric rubbed his jaw, when he actually wanted to slap his own cheeks. Perhaps submerge his head in a bucket of icy water.

No matter how hard he tried to concentrate on the words of Oliver, his steward, or Larkin, his chamberlain, his attention kept moving to Evaine. It should be impossible for any scent to be so clear in a Great Hall with five hundred wolves, countless platters of food, four roaring fireplaces, plus a passel of musicians. Yet he could smell her like the headiest of wines, even though Evaine stood with his mother on the other side of the hall, a ridiculously great distance away. She was, quite objectively, the most beautiful female in England. Really, such loveliness couldn't be improved upon, but his fingers itched to drape her in ermine, or see her naked once more wearing naught but diamonds.

To see her flushed and sated in his bed, her inner thighs sticky with her own honey and his seed...yet already craving him again...

"My king?"

Alaric nearly jumped a foot in the air. "Beg pardon, Oliver?"

His steward peered at him, brow furrowed. "You groaned. Are you ill? I can have Blanche prepare a tonic."

"No," Alaric ground out. "I'm quite well, do not trouble your mate. Forgive me, it is overloud in here. You were speaking about an upcoming hunt?'

Oliver graciously repeated all the details regarding a planned fallow deer hunt, and mentioned a few wooden fence repairs that could not be delayed until spring. Yet Alaric was scarcely able to confirm instructions and dismiss the retainer before his attention diverted once again, to Evaine walking toward him. She progressed slowly; now that most tables had been cleared away, many in his pack were stopping to introduce themselves, but each step closer she came, his shoulders relaxed further.

Alaric took a deep breath and turned to his chamberlain. "Now, Larkin. What was your question?"

The younger wolf, whose father had served Alaric's sire in the same position dedicated solely to the wellbeing of the king and his family, inclined his head. "Did you have any special instructions for this evening, my king? Regarding...linen or refreshments?"

Goddess. Larkin wanted to know if his king would be taking anyone to bed after the banquet so he could prepare the royal bedchamber accordingly. Over the years Alaric had been asked the question countless times in other castles, manors, even inns, because so many she-wolves wished to say they had bedded a king. However, since his great misfortune with Theda, he politely declined or offered vague excuses, the required steps in that blade-edge dance of pleasing or offending a host. Tonight, he yearned to order a complete linen change. And a tray holding supper and wine for two.

No. Evaine is not your mate. She is royalty with a bounty on her head, given sanctuary in your castle. Stop this madness.

Yes. She nearly touched herself at the high table! Now that she is recovering from her ordeal, the princess is awakening to a grown wolf's lust and requires a discreet tutor. You could be that tutor...

Alaric scowled as the two thoughts warred relentlessly, one factual and rational, the other irrational and foolish. But he had to be the former. That was the lot of a diplomat, even a kingly one.

"No," Alaric said eventually. "No special instructions. Actually, I might retire to my library soon and leave the elder queen to lead the dancing, for I have a great pile of documents to read. I would appreciate fresh candles in there, the fire stoked, and some wine. I fear it will be a long night."

Larkin hesitated. "If you change your mind, just send for me. I serve in the best interests of the crown, always."

The words hardly needed to be said; few positions held as much trust and influence as a chamberlain, due to their close proximity to the royal family. But they were appreciated all the same, and Alaric smiled as Larkin bowed then darted away to complete his tasks.

"You're leaving?" said Evaine as she approached, her gaze traveling up and down his form as though assessing him for injury.

"I am quite well," he replied hastily, albeit unsure why the need to reassure her was so important. "Just a small mountain of documents to read, including Henry's ducal edict."

She lifted one delicate eyebrow. "And that must be done tonight?"

No.

Just for a moment, Alaric feared he'd said the word aloud. Inexplicably, his much-vaunted skills, such as the ability to speak and reveal nothing at all, vanished when around Princess Evaine de Wynter.

"I merely desire a little peace and quiet," he said eventually. "In my library."

Evaine smiled. "I wish to return to my bedchamber. Will you escort me?"

Goddess.

Already he could imagine Evaine, naked in front of the fireplace, attending to an evening sponge bath. The warmed water would trickle down her luscious form, anointing those sweet pink nipples and gather in the tangle of blond hair crowning her mound. But she would linger with the sponge between her legs. Rub it back and forth, moaning softly at the burgeoning pleasure...

"King Alaric?" she repeated, a little impatiently.

Damnation. Clearly, he needed to be slapped out of his lust stupor. Not Wesley, for the squire would roll about the floor laughing if asked. Captain Bardolf? He had meaty fists and would administer a proper skull-shaker.

"Of course," Alaric ground out, offering his arm. "Let us depart before we are waylaid further. Mother will host in my absence; she loves to dance and will still be twirling long after most are exhausted. I think only my father could persuade her from the floor."

Unexpectedly, Evaine grinned as they strolled toward the hall entrance, nodding at various courtiers in farewell. "I'm sure he had methods of persuasion that others did not."

"Do not remind me," he groaned as they proceeded down the wide torchlit hallway. "Those two were insatiable, even as elder wolves. I will remain forever grateful for Blackstone's thick, sturdy walls, especially in rutting season..."

Alaric's voice trailed off, his cheeks flushing as once again his mouth formed words his mind had not given permission to express. For someone so experienced in diplomacy, the way his tongue loosened around Evaine was entirely unnerving.

Pressing his lips together as they passed two armed guards and ascended the spiral staircase to the royal apartments, Alaric inwardly vowed to remain silent until Evaine was safely in her chamber.

Except then the she-wolf smiled sweetly, batted her lashes, and said: "Tell me about *rutting season*."

Leto have mercy.

Alaric swallowed hard as his cock twitched. "You know that mated she-wolves can only conceive between January and March, and if they do, cubs are born in May?"

Somehow, her smile grew even sweeter. "Of course, but I feel like there are so many other details to share. *Interesting* details."

Perspiration broke out on his temples. "Cubs are very precious because so many stars must align. It's not just the time of year—she-wolves mated with a male must also go into a week-long breeding heat. That doesn't always happen. But if it does, for seven days they, ah..."

"Rut?" said Evaine, her green eyes glinting. "Anytime, anywhere?"

"Yes," he growled. "But a she-wolf's breeding heat is so powerful, it affects the entire castle. Most feel the lust. The need. A king must be lenient, for he is liable to come across rutting in the most unexpected of places. Alcoves. Privy chambers. Staircases. Against tree trunks. Crushing Cook's herbs in the garden. Dangling over a damned rampart..."

She giggled, then bit her lip. "And you, King Alaric? Do you feel the lust? The need?"

Until you arrived at my castle...no. Now it is the only thing on my mind.

After a thousand-year walk, they finally reached Evaine's chamber. He'd never been more relieved to see a door in all his life; a few more steps and he'd have confessed all his raw, carnal thoughts. "Here we are, princess. Your chamber. I hope you enjoyed the banquet, and wish you a good evening."

Evaine stared at him, her gaze searching. Then she dipped into a low curtsy. "Thank you for the escort. Good evening."

Once the chamber door shut, Alaric took a long, slow breath. Then he hurried to his library, carefully closing the door behind him before marching over to the fireplace and resting both hands on the carved stone mantel. He wasn't sure how long he stared at the flames, desperate to regain control. But in the blink of an eye he'd removed his doublet, unfastened his hose, and gripped his aching cock. The swollen head was already wet with seed and Alaric used it to ease his way, gliding his palm up and down the thick length, squeezing roughly with his fingers.

He groaned, his mind betraying him once more as it offered the portrait of a naked Evaine on her hands and knees in front of him, her thighs spread wide to reveal her glistening center.

"Yes," Alaric muttered, his hand moving faster. "Show me that sweet cunt. Is it burning to be filled, Evie? Do you need my cock so deep you feel it in your soul?"

"Yes. Yes, I do."

Horror flooded him at the soft words. Yet as he turned his head, no matter how hard he willed it to be untrue, two facts remained. Evaine stood in his library in a linen night-gown and heavy brocade robe, her hair flowing around her shoulders. And he'd quite literally been caught with his hose around his knees, handling his engorged cock.

"What are you doing in here?" Alaric roared. "My private rooms? Did you not consider knocking?"

Her emerald gaze never leaving his, Evaine untied the sash around her waist and let the robe fall to the floor. "I did consider it, yes. But then I'd have missed a most magnificent sight. As to my purpose...I'm pouncing."

"*Pouncing*?" Alaric repeated, solely for time to regather his thoughts. His senses demanded he tear the offensively modest nightgown from her exquisite form so he might view her once again.

"Indeed," she replied, straightening her shoulders, before awkwardly removing the remaining garment and tossing it away, the most erotic disrobing he'd ever witnessed. "Since you so rudely abandoned me in my bedchamber, I decided to invade your library. I've waited long enough, Alaric. Pleasure me."

E vaine gulped in tiny, panting breaths as she waited for Alaric to respond to her outrageous demand.

As a cub she'd been known as Evaine the Bold, yet it had taken more courage than she'd thought possible to leave her bedchamber and walk to the king's library. However, she'd then seen a sight now seared in her mind for eternity: Alaric, half-naked, touching himself.

Thinking of her so intently he'd given her a nickname.

Show me that sweet cunt. Is it burning to be filled, Evie? Do you need my cock so deep you feel it in your soul?

Only such raw, lusty words could have provoked her to disrobe. But although she stood naked, the chilly night air caressing her skin, Alaric's glittering gaze might ensure she never felt cold again.

"Well?" she said imperiously, folding her arms and tapping her foot, but her gaze kept returning to the tempting sight of his huge bobbing cock. What would it be like to hold that length in her hands? To stroke it? And the pearly fluid coating the swollen, almost purple head...what did that taste like?

A slow smile curled Alaric's lips as he removed his hose, revealing long, heavily muscled legs. Then he prowled toward her, a hunter, an alpha male, every inch King of the Western Lands. "You dare to hide your breasts from me?" he said slowly as he circled her. "I forbid it."

"Oh?" Evaine replied unsteadily, as his dark, delicious scent wrapped itself around her like a cloak, hardening her nipples and provoking a gush of moisture between her thighs. "You *forbid* it? Someone alert the realm!"

"Do you know what happens to saucy-tongued princesses?" said Alaric as he halted behind her, so close she could feel the heat of his fire-warmed skin. Then one big hand pressed against the middle of her back.

Branding her.

Evaine whimpered, her arms falling to her sides, and her breasts thrusting forward, high and proud.

How does he have such power over me?

Involuntarily, her hips circled and her arse brushed against his cock.

Alaric groaned and she felt the moment he succumbed to need, oh-so-briefly grinding himself against her. Then his hand moved, sliding up her spine until it gripped her neck. To someone else it might have been a frightening hold, yet Evaine smiled as a rush of heady delight flooded through her. He was attempting to keep her still to regain control. While this mighty wolf king already commanded her body, he was equally affected by the heat between them.

"Why, Alaric," she purred, circling her hips deliberately this time, rubbing her arse against the stone-like shaft pressing against her. "Does it hurt to be that hard? To want me so very much?"

A low growl rumbled in his chest, and without thinking,

71

Evaine spread her thighs. Such a raw, primitive sound demanded it.

Now, he chuckled, his hand moving away from her neck to slide down and cup her right breast. After rubbing his thumb back and forth across her nipple he pinched it, the brief pain sizzling directly to her core.

Evaine moaned.

"Poor princess," he crooned as his strong fingers tormented the tender peak to throbbing sensitivity. Then he did the same to her left breast. "I wonder what you need most? For me to suck those pretty pink nipples until they are the color of wine...or to stroke between your legs? You're so wet. It must ache terribly."

"Call me Evie," she gasped. "Not princess. I like Evie... oh..."

Her eyes closed briefly as his mouth trailed across her shoulder, his teeth lightly scraping her sensitive skin. The gentle, almost affectionate kiss was a stark contrast to his gloriously rough treatment of her nipples, far too much for her swirling mind. Then his hand continued down, over her ribs and belly, halting just at the top of her mound.

How dare he stop!

Her eyes flew open at the unacceptable teasing and she jerked her hips, blatantly attempting to move his hand to the spot where she needed it most.

"Very well...*Evie*," Alaric growled, although he sounded pleased rather than annoyed. "If you wish me to touch your cunt...beg for it."

Beg? A royal she-wolf? He was quite mad.

"There will be snow in summer before I do so...ohhh," said Evaine, as his fingers brushed the thicket of crisp curls between her thighs, agonizingly close to her swollen pleasure bud, but skating past it to caress her inner thighs. "*Alaric...*"

"Something to say?"

Words? He wanted words? How could she reply when she scarcely knew which way was up? Nothing mattered right now but easing that relentless ache.

"Pleasure me," Evaine choked out. "Immediately."

"I want to, very much," he replied lazily, as his fingertips swirled a pattern on her inner thighs and his tongue flicked the side of her neck. "There is nothing I'd like more than to hear your scream of pleasure, to feel your sweet honey drench my fingers. But I haven't heard the necessary entreaty."

She trembled, her body feverish, her entire world reduced to one need. If she didn't spend, she would surely die. "What must I say? Tell me. Tell me exactly."

As though offering approval, his fingertips began circling back up toward her mound, his thumb knuckle parting her bush. "Just three little words, Evie...*please, my king.*"

"Please...my king."

His feral snarl filled her with a giddy joy, but Alaric was a benevolent conqueror, his thumb swiftly moving to tease her pleasure bud.

Evaine cried out. Surely nothing in the world could feel this good.

"Oh, you like that, beautiful Evie?" Alaric growled as he kissed her shoulder. "What else do you need? My fingers inside that burning hot cunt?"

"Do it," she gasped. "I can't bear the ache. Please. *Please.*"

Alaric didn't say a word, but his big hand roughly cupped her mound. Claiming possession. Claiming *her*.

Next, two thick fingers eased inside her wet heat and Evaine writhed as her untouched channel was stretched for the first time. Greedy for more, the sensation of fullness, the light friction, she pressed against his hand...and cried out again as his fingertip rubbed against a spot so sensitive that she bucked against him.

"There?" Alaric asked, sounding exceedingly smug.

Evaine scowled. If she didn't crave more of this divine stroking, she would have crushed his instep. How could she retaliate and level the scales? "Touch yourself," she whispered. "Stroke your cock while you pleasure me."

He inhaled unsteadily. "Not just saucy-tongued, but lusty as well. How to manage such a wicked princess?"

"You can but try," she said simply, her head falling back against his massive chest as his fingers thrust inside her, his thumb teasing her pleasure bud until she thought she might scream. Something was building inside her, building and building like a rock gathering speed as it tumbled down a hill.

Desperate to discover, Evaine ground her mound against him. Yet moments later it was all so much better, so much hotter, when his knuckles scraped against her arse, the smooth, silken weight of his heavy cockhead slapping against her skin as he handled himself. Their combined scents, her wetness, his seed, the light sheen of sweat and desire were dizzying, but his fingers were nothing short of magical. How did he know exactly the depth to plunge them? How to twist just a little when he rubbed so it felt like her whole channel was being caressed? And the pressure on her swollen bud...nearly perfect, but...

She whimpered.

"Tell me, sweetheart," Alaric rasped in her ear.

"Faster," Evaine moaned. "Harder. I want...I want...I *need*..."

She could scarcely speak, yet somehow, he knew. With the heel of his hand pressing firmly against her mound, Alaric added a third finger. Evaine gasped at the luscious impalement, the erotic sensation of being held up solely by his fingers and entirely at his mercy, exactly what she craved. Then he knitted the three together and twisted them, rubbing against that internal spot that made her writhe.

"Yes," snarled Alaric into her ear as he bit her shoulder. "Spend for me, sweetheart. I want to hear your pleasure. I want everyone to hear it. You're so beautiful. So lusty. And the way your sweet cunt is gripping my fingers...*Goddess*..."

The wicked words tumbled her over the edge. Bucking against him, Evaine opened her mouth and unleashed a sound she didn't even know she possessed: a long, guttural howl of pure ecstasy. Shortly afterward he roared, and hot seed lashed across her lower back. But that wasn't enough, for Alaric smeared it over her skin. An act of pure possession.

Evaine sighed in complete contentment as she sagged against him, panting for breath. Yet then she went rigid as a shocking pain seared across the back of her neck. "Ow. Ow!"

"Evie?" said Alaric, his concern unmistakable as he carefully withdrew his fingers. "Are you sore? Is this too much?"

"My neck," she replied, wincing and lifting a hand to swipe at it.

Wait. What was that?

"Alaric," she continued, now alarmed. "Can you see anything under my hair? It feels rough. Bumpy."

He gingerly lifted her hair. "No. *No!*"

"What? What is it?"

There was a long, long silence. So long, Evaine trembled in fear. Then one blunt finger traced a shape over and over, as though he didn't understand either.

"It's two stars," said Alaric eventually, in a tone she'd never heard him use. One of utter confusion...and a little wonder. "Above that, a crown."

Evaine froze. She'd just seen those symbols! "The royal mating mark? My mother had that mark on her nape. Your mother does, too. My father had it on his wrist."

He stepped back, and the distance felt like a chasm, the cool air now making her shiver.

"But this cannot be," Alaric said hoarsely. "I'm already mated and she is *dead*."

———

Still reeling, Alaric struggled to regather his scattered senses.

Pleasuring Evaine, drowning in their combined scents, hearing the most perfect sound imaginable: the long, strong howl of a she-wolf finding sweet release because of his touch, then staking his claim and spending all over her soft skin...nothing could be more satisfying. It had all felt so right here in his library, the place where they'd first met.

But the royal fated mate mark suddenly appearing on the nape of her neck had shocked him to the core. The symbols had risen so swiftly after Evaine reached her peak. With Theda, he had no idea when it happened; as he'd woken with heavy limbs and a foggy head, the mark had just been there. But the two stars and crown looked very different on Evaine—a flawless celestial blue against her creamy skin, the lines so precise and even, as though they'd been stamped by Leto herself. Whereas Theda's neck—and his wrist—had been mottled pink with inflammation, the lines a little rough and the color noticeably lighter.

Because they'd been etched.

Had Theda chosen a sleeping draught to dull her pain? Or was it only him who'd been drugged?

Alaric pressed a closed fist to his lips, unsure whether to roar, rampage through the castle, or simply sit and rock with mad laughter until some kind soul dumped icy water over his head. How terribly humiliating it was to concede that he'd been so easily and neatly caught in a trap.

"Alaric?" said Evaine softly, jolting him from the cage of his chaotic thoughts. "I can see you are sorely troubled. Talk to me."

He rubbed his jaw. As a diplomat, as a king, he always had the words to reassure or explain. Yet right now he was as muddled and uncertain as a traveler newly arrived on foreign shores. "Forgive me. I know...I know I have ruined something special—"

"Nothing is ruined," Evaine countered, her gaze steady in the bright glow of the well-lit library. "As long as I understand what is in your heart."

Everything within urged him to step forward and hold her close. But naked Evie was far too tempting and the words that needed to be said were far too important. "I feel like I'm crossing the marshlands blindfolded, with no damned clue if my next step will be solid ground or swamp to suck me under. I truly thought I was mated already. But it was all a lie. Your mark is genuine, but I had to watch it happen to know the difference."

Her brow furrowed. "How so?"

Alaric gritted his teeth and looked away. "I met Theda at a banquet in Gloucester. My father had recently passed, my mother was in seclusion, and I felt no desire for revelry. But I'd promised to attend. She was the daughter of a noble family. We danced, drank wine...well, I drank and she fetched more. One particular goblet tasted a little different, but she urged me to finish it swiftly then gestured to the door...next thing I remember, I woke up in her chamber with a mating mark on my wrist and her soothsayer demanding I crown her queen without delay. Word spread across the realm before I could even take a breath...but everyone was so *happy* at the thought of a mating ceremony and the prospect of heirs. Even Mother was pleased, initially...so I did it."

"That wretched imposter tricked you while you were *grieving*," said Evaine slowly. "Such evil is almost unfathomable. How very Hera-like. Theda and her accomplices must have planned that very carefully. An invitation, a sleeping potion, an etcher, her soothsayer arriving at just the right time."

"It never felt quite right. But I didn't believe I deserved better, after...after being away from Blackstone when Father passed. I was judging some foolish dispute in Cardiff, thinking myself very grand and important. I should have been *here*. Some part of me knew he wasn't long for this earth, but I thought I had time. I didn't. When Leto calls a faithful servant home to glory amongst the stars, nothing can change that," finished Alaric, his heart heavy. Even now, the grief, the regret, was almost impossible to bear.

Yet when a soft, cool hand curled itself around his, somehow the load on his shoulders lightened. The healing magic of a simple touch.

"I remember when they came to visit," said Evaine. "King Cyrus had silver hair even then. But he was so kind and his eyes *twinkled*. He adored your mother, and whenever anyone asked a question, he'd always say '*Queen Siân knows best*'."

A reluctant chuckle escaped his lips. "Do you know Father tried to deny himself and her, insisting they couldn't possibly be a match because he was so much older? Fortunately, Mother knew who her mate was."

"And pounced on him in a stable," said Evaine. "She advised me not to follow her lead, as straw was a dreadful bother to remove from clothing and hair."

Alaric almost choked. "Mother never confessed that particular detail! Everyone thinks she's so lofty and regal... they've never seen her dance 'til dawn barefoot, or drag Father from a meeting for kisses. But his passing broke her and I didn't know how to offer comfort. How do you comfort the loss of a fated mate? It is unendurable. She went into seclusion, I was trying to be king and establish a new order in the pack, quell challenges from a few cousins... then came the Gloucester banquet."

"Evil," Evaine hissed, flashing her fangs. "Now I understand why Queen Siân was so wary about my arrival. I suppose Theda was Lady Innocent? Pure and untouchable?"

He flushed. "I thought I knew how to dissemble, so politely, so smoothly, that no one could ever be offended. Also how to lie and flatter to best advantage, the true currency of a diplomat. But I was a babe in the woods compared to Theda and her soothsayer, Silas. They moved me about like a damned chess piece. I thought I would never trust again."

"Did you ever share your suspicions?" Evaine asked.

Alaric shook his head. "I couldn't. In truth I couldn't even admit it to myself. But looking back, there were other clues. Theda had a pleasant-enough flowery scent, but it never inflamed me, never made me want to *pounce*. Wesley could smell her also. Theda hated my squire and was always cruel, forever banishing him from our presence. That was why. Goddess, even now I can remember the raised hackles between Blanche and Theda. And Mother and Theda. They saw under her mask...but after a public mating ceremony and crowning, it can only be undone by death. I still don't know why Theda did it, other than wanting power at any cost."

"Because, my king, in a poisoned soul, power is a thirst that can never be quenched. But if Theda hadn't passed, I would scratch her eyes out. For her lies. For hurting you. For touching what is mine."

Alaric blinked at the sheer fierceness of the words. His petite princess indeed looked ready to do murder, and a new but peaceful feeling of warmth flooded him. "Yours?"

Evaine straightened her shoulders, her perfect breasts jutting forward in a way that made his supposedly spent cock jerk to attention. Then she met his gaze, those glorious de Wynter green eyes glittering, and placed her hand in the middle of his chest. "*Mine.*"

He sucked in a breath as an eye-watering pain slashed across his inner wrist, like he'd been seared with a hot poker. Shockingly, his etched mark disappeared, like mud wiped from glass. A moment later the symbols of a true royal mating mark rose on his skin, identical in every way to those on Evaine's nape.

"Goddess," Alaric whispered, abruptly torn between wrapping himself around his mate to imprint more of him on her...and waking every single wolf in the Western Lands to show them his mark.

This was *real*. Princess Evaine de Wynter was his fated

mate, and future anointed Queen of the Western Lands. Perhaps, Leto willing, even the mother of his cubs. Indeed, a whole new horizon stretched out ahead of him. One with endless possibilities.

A low growl of complete satisfaction rumbled in his chest, and Evaine whimpered. "You are aware that sound makes me very, very wet?"

Inhaling deeply, Alaric smiled. "It seems so...*my mate*. But I shall have to examine the situation more closely, on my desk."

She trembled, her nipples jewel-hard, then poked her tongue out. "You'll have to catch me first!"

Lust surged through him as Evaine darted across the library to the shelves of books, before halting to wiggle her arse, looking over her shoulder and winking. This she-wolf was perfection.

Alaric permitted the pretense of a hunt for a short while, his low growls echoing in the room as she teased him, tweaking her own nipples, even caressing her bush. But soon the need to taste Evaine's soaked cunt overruled all else. He trapped his mate against the desk, lifting her up onto the polished oak surface.

Gathering her hair in one fist, Alaric tugged until Evaine arched her back, offering him those sweet breasts. "Do you concede, Evie?" he rasped, lashing one tender peak with his tongue then blowing softly.

She gasped. "A royal she-wolf concede? Ha...ohhhh..."

Alaric laughed against her silken skin as he continued tormenting her nipples, circling with his tongue and lightly scoring with his teeth. "If you think this feels good, imagine my tongue inside you."

"Then take me...my king."

The words would forever inflame him. With a feral

snarl, he gripped the back of Evaine's neck and kissed her deeply, mastering her petal-soft lips before plunging his tongue into her mouth. But she was no passive receiver, winding her arms about his neck and tangling her tongue with his.

He groaned, only breaking the kiss when catching his breath seemed impossible. But the call of her drenched center was far too strong. "Spread your thighs, sweetheart. I'm going to kiss your cunt."

———

If she could capture a moment in time it would be this one: Alaric gazing at her with such desire, such possessiveness... yet also something much deeper, like she was dawn after an endless night.

He was her fated mate; they had the marks to prove it. Now he would teach her so much more about pleasure.

Evaine leaned back on her hands, bringing her feet up to the edge of the desk for balance and offering him a long look at her drenched center. Then she teased him by immediately pressing her thighs back together. It made Alaric's eyes flash, and his growl of warning made her wetter than ever. Indeed, she might be a strong and bold she-wolf, but there was something so exciting about provoking her alpha king until he dominated her thoroughly. "Perhaps I spoke too soon. Surely a reward is much sweeter when one battles for it...my king."

Without warning she was flat on her back, the smooth, polished wood of the desk cool against her fevered skin. His muscled forearms curled around her spread thighs, anchoring her in place. "That saucy tongue, Evaine," Alaric rumbled, as he leaned down to inhale deeply of her scent, before blowing gently on her bush, ruffling the crisp hair.

Before, he'd kissed her with unleashed passion. Now the cool, calm king had returned, the one who would torment her until she begged for release.

Evaine moaned, attempting to lift her hips so she might grind her throbbing, aching center against his chin, or even better, be closer for his tongue.

But her mate merely laughed. "Now, what were you saying about rewards being sweeter when one battles for it, Evie?"

"*Alaric.*"

"I must confess," he said conversationally, as though they were two humans discussing the weather, "if I knew no other scent than your wet cunt until the end of time, I would be quite content. It is like earth and air and water and fire and honey cakes combined. Sweet and musky."

"Then taste me," Evaine pleaded. "Take me. Give me what I need."

Alaric pulled back slightly, his thick brows drawing together. "*Take you?* Not until we are publicly mated and you are crowned Queen of the Western Lands. Such ceremonies take many weeks to prepare, perhaps as long as a month..."

Her outrage almost unleashed like a storm...until she saw his faint lip twitch. He was teasing her once more.

Evaine nodded slowly, then languidly lifted a hand to cup her right breast, lifting and weighing it, stroking it, before lightly pinching her own nipple. "Mmmm...you are right of course. A month. Yes, so many things to prepare. Fine clothing and jewels, a full banquet and entertainment, invitations to dignitaries, offerings to Leto..."

Alaric's searing gaze fixed on her hand's movements. "Tomorrow."

She giggled, pinching her nipple with more force. "Ooooh. Certainly not. The tapestry with both royal crests must be embroidered. We'll need colored flags for the ramparts. And your soothsayer needs time to arrange the ceremony. Two weeks."

"Three days," he responded, tracing her inner thigh with the tip of his tongue.

Goddess. How is anyone supposed to think when their mate does that?

"One week," Evaine managed breathlessly. "We must have a proper ceremony that welcomes the future and honors the past, Alaric."

"One week," he agreed, his eyes glinting, and a part of her just *knew* that had been his intention all along. Wicked wolf!

She batted her lashes at him. "Now, are you going to do what you promised, or must I find someone else...oh!"

Evaine bucked as Alaric nuzzled the crisp hair between her legs, parting it slightly and nudging the swollen bud nestled there. Then, balancing on his elbows, he used his thumbs to spread her glistening nether petals.

"Watch me," he growled. "Watch me *feast*."

At the first touch of his rough tongue on her pleasure bud, Evaine moaned at the jolt that lanced through her entire body. But as he laved and nipped, as he circled the nub then took it into his mouth and suckled, she could only thrash atop the desk as once more that wave of heady sensation built and built. Without warning it exploded, and she cried out his name as bliss crashed over her.

Yet he didn't stop. Alaric merely moved down a little and began lapping up the honey trickling from her center.

On a few occasions she'd heard human women whisper about the delights of a lover's mouth, but surely nothing in the world could compare to Alaric's tongue. The roughness. The dexterity. The *hunger*. Even better, the strength and force as he plunged it inside her channel, entering and withdrawing and rubbing and flicking...

Evaine's fingers tangled in Alaric's thick hair as she held him in place, never wanting this perfect pleasuring of her needy core to end. She might not be able to move her legs, but as he hurled her toward ecstasy a second time, her hips bounced on the desk, her toes gripped the edge, and she screamed as she found her peak once more.

Panting for air, her mind empty in a most peaceful way, Evaine sighed happily. "Is it Western Land lore that a mate must use his tongue at least every other day? If not, then you must rewrite it at once."

Alaric chuckled, but there was a certain tension in the sound that made her lift her head. Oh. Her mate's golden eyes glowed, his mouth and chin were slick with her honey...but there were lines of strain on his rugged face, and a brief glance downward explained why. Once again, his cock bobbed against his belly, huge and dark pink, the swollen head dripping with seed.

Evaine tilted her head as she studied the thick shaft, smiling to herself as it seemed to grow even larger. Watching him handle it as he thought of her, of feeling him spend on her lower back had been fascinating enough. But now her mouth watered to taste that seed. To know what his smooth, heavy length felt like in her hand. Between her lips. "You pleasured me. I think it is only fair that I do the same."

An expression of pure yearning flashed across his face. "You don't have to."

A tart reply sprang to her lips, then Evaine hesitated. *The imposter queen.* If Theda had rejected or avoided Alaric's touch...it was highly unlikely she'd ever sank to her knees in front of him and kissed his cock. Made him *roar*.

But Evaine de Wynter, his true fated mate, would pleasure him senseless.

Excitement sizzled through her. Sitting up, Evaine carefully slid off the desk. Her legs were a little unsteady, but she remained standing. "Lean against the desk please, Alaric. I'll just fetch a cushion. Stone floors aren't good for knees."

Alaric inhaled unsteadily, and she could practically feel his hungry stare burning her back as she crossed the library to fetch a velvet cushion from the chaise by the window. Unable to stop herself, Evaine wiggled her arse again, somehow swallowing a giggle at his helpless growl. He might be a lofty king with the most magical tongue in Wolfdom, but she still held a great deal of power. After so many years of having none whatsoever, it felt *wonderful*.

With her hips swaying and breasts bobbing, Evaine returned to the desk, dropped the cushion onto the floor, then gracefully knelt upon it.

Alaric cleared his throat. "As I said...you don't have to do this."

Leaning forward, Evaine inhaled the delicious scent of him, all hot and raw and carnal. "Oh, but I want to kiss your cock, my king. Kiss and suck it until you spend in my mouth."

He groaned, taking her hand and wrapping it around his engorged length, before placing both his palms on the edge of the desk. "Touch me, Evie. However you want."

Well. Cocks were indeed *fascinating*.

Examining it closely, Evaine glided her palm along his

length, marveling at the contrast of soft, smooth skin over stone-hard core. And his cock was hot. Scorching hot! Even more curious now, she tightened her grip.

Alaric cursed, his knuckles near-white, but his hands remained on the desk.

Mischievously, she met his gaze, then stuck out her tongue and licked the wet head. Hmmm. The pearly fluid tasted salty and a little earthy. Fascinating! "Like that?"

Her powerful alpha mate actually trembled. "Just like that."

Heady excitement surged through Evaine, and she traced the delicate lines on his shaft with just the tip of her tongue until the sound of creaking wood startled her out of her cock-trance. Oh dear. If she kept teasing him, Alaric might actually crush his oak desk to powder.

Taking pity on her mate—and the desk—Evaine peered up at Alaric. "Guide my head."

Then she closed her lips around his cock and drew upon it.

"Goddess, yes," breathed Alaric as he cupped the back of her head, gently directing her. "Can you take me a little deeper? Ah, that's it, my clever sweetheart. You feel so good. So. Damned. Good."

Warmed by the praise, wanting to please her mate, Evaine dared to suck him further into her mouth, hollowing her cheeks to increase the suction, her tongue flicking against the underside. His hips jerked, his hand gripped her hair tightly, and a feral snarl tore from his throat. Her Alaric was unraveling.

Greedily, she sucked harder, then lifted her hand to caress his heavy balls. While she was nearly choking on the huge length, her eyes actually watering, it was so very intoxicating to hear his unabashed pleasure, to watch him surrender to her ministrations. Then his head fell back and his roar of release nearly lifted the castle roof as seed gushed into her mouth.

After swallowing it all, Evaine neatly licked him clean, then sat back on her heels. "My king."

Alaric cupped her cheek, then tucked a stray lock of hair behind her ear. "One week, not a heartbeat longer. Then everyone will know my queen. My mate. Forever."

CHAPTER
FIVE

With all the preparation required for a royal mating ceremony and queen-crowning, Alaric had been certain that a week would pass faster than a tail twitch.

Ha. How utterly wrong.

Scowling darkly, Alaric stared into the flickering flames warming his library. It seemed like a thousand years since he and Evaine had pleasured each other in this very room, but it had only been three days. Three endless days of making lists, sending invitations, approving menus and cloth and other expenditure, and being measured for the traditional and exceedingly elaborate crowning ceremony garments. Oliver had also hired more wolves to sew and cook and hunt so Blackstone Castle would be ready for an onslaught of honored guests, including his brother kings Ranulf and Darius.

Apart from the birth of an heir, nothing was more important in wolf society than a royal mating ceremony. It announced the beginning of a new cycle, at times, the rise of a new pack, and set the stage for future stability and peace in the land—or disorder and strife. It was an occasion where significant diplomacy took place; bargains were struck, disputes resolved, the state of the realm discussed in libraries, solars, and great halls alike. Of course, some wished to attend only because such a large gathering offered a stronger chance of meeting a fated mate. Others merely wanted to enjoy the entertainment and indulge in endless food and drink.

While only a select few witnessed the official mating ceremony, Evaine would be crowned in front of his pack on a specially constructed dais in the large castle courtyard. They would sit for a formal portrait sketch, which would later become an oil painting to be hung in the gallery. After their guests had been farewelled and returned home, he and Evaine would then lead a royal procession from the castle and spend a full month traveling around the Western Lands. This was an opportunity for all his subjects to kneel to their new anointed queen, and receive gifts of gold buckles or hair combs to commemorate the occasion.

Alaric sighed. Really, in this matter, they weren't so different to humans. Except royal wolves were infinitely harder to kill.

Just briefly, his fangs and claws elongated. Only yesterday, one of his guards had brought word of a bloody tussle between villagers and a pack of outcasts on the road from Bewdley. While no one had been killed, two aspects had greatly concerned him: the ever-increasing size of the roaming pack...and how close they had ventured to Blackstone Castle. Within five miles!

Were the outcasts just hot-tempered, looking to fight anyone? Foreign wolves looking to establish a new territory? Or most concerning: were they actually mercenaries with one purpose, to collect the substantial bounty on Evaine's head?

Alaric curled a fist and thumped it against the carved stone mantel. If anyone so much as *looked* upon his queen without reverence, there would be no leniency. No mercy. He would execute without regret.

"My king? Might I have a word?"

Alaric turned his head and beckoned Oliver into the library. His steward looked ready to heave everyone over the ramparts; entirely understandable given the circumstances. Planning and preparing for such an important event, one that would be spoken of for many years to come, and involve the presence of England's royal packs, would turn any steward's fur white. Not to mention this was the *second* time he'd had to do it. "What troubles you? Are you concerned about the outcasts?"

Oliver huffed out a breath. "I'm sure everyone is concerned about them, but I have decided to leave that particular burden to Captain Bardolf. He sent out another hunting party this morning; if the outcasts have come to the Western Lands with evil intent, Leto willing, our guards will return with a bulging satchel of fresh hearts to be burned."

"Indeed," said Alaric grimly. "I will tolerate no disturbance around my future queen. Not even a playful fight. Evaine is *mine*. She is...well, you understand."

The steward actually smiled a little. "We all understand, my king. While it was certainly shocking to learn Lady Theda wasn't your true mate, everyone is joyful beyond words about Princess Evaine. What it means for you. What it means for the Western Lands. Poor Larkin can barely move his fingers, he's written so many letters. But, er, well...fated mates is why I am here. It is now January, and the start of rutting season. I don't believe we've ever had a royal mating ceremony within this month. Have we, er...procedures to follow if our new queen, or perhaps other mated she-wolves, go into their breeding heat early while the castle is overflowing with guests? I know the risk is low, but...well, you never know."

Alaric nodded slowly. It was an excellent and pertinent question. As he'd mentioned to Evaine, rutting season could turn even the most sensible wolves into feral beasts. It only took one mated she-wolf in the vicinity to go into breeding heat, and everyone in or near the castle would absorb that lust and run mad with it. His own pack would be enough for the guards and himself to manage. But with hundreds of guests...or if it were Evaine pouncing on him, demanding his cock, his tongue, his seed, all day and all night...

Goddess.

What if Evie was chosen? If she went into heat and conceived, there might be cubs in May, that most sacred of months, for it heralded an increasingly rare miracle in Wolfdom: new life. Leto had fought so hard to birth Apollo and Artemis, and this Hera-driven difficulty had continued on over the centuries. Between all the wars, mercenaries, and ancient restrictions around conceiving, the English wolf shifter population was steadily dwindling. But he and Evaine still had a chance to experience something very special. The birth of a cub. Perhaps even more than one. A litter!

Alaric swayed, actually having to reach out to the mantel to steady himself.

"My king?" said Oliver anxiously. "Forgive the impertinent question."

"It wasn't impertinent, but important," replied Alaric carefully. "I just...it just hit me fully that this year it might be *me* caring for my mate in her heat."

Oliver's whole expression changed into one of warmth and humor. "Leto willing, you'll know that blessed exhaustion, my king. Your sire generously gave me several days to recover both times with Blanche. She was...er... fierce."

Now Alaric laughed. "I can only imagine."

"I believe your sire required a week—"

"Stop! I beg you," said Alaric, his shoulders shaking. Goddess, laughter felt good. It seemed he'd laughed and smiled more since meeting Evaine than all his years before that.

The difference of a fated mate.

Oliver beamed. "Do you have instructions, though? Naturally you will care for Her Highness should it be required, but what of a guest or pack member? One just never knows once the season begins."

"A truth. Prepare two of the old hunting lodges, the ones down by the river. Fresh linens and firewood, the kitchens can easily supply food and drink if necessary. But if any female goes into her breeding heat, she and her mate must be escorted straight there. I cannot risk an entire castle losing their wits."

"Very good," said the steward, inclining his head. "Now, I—"

"Beg pardon, my king," said a guard, as he rushed into the room without knocking, his face flushed pink from the frigid cold outside.

Both Alaric and Oliver went still.

"Yes?" said Alaric brusquely, his heart beginning to pound. What now? Another fight with outcasts? A mercenary attack? Some sort of written threat?

The guard mopped his brow with a sleeve. "A carriage pulled up at the bridge with a couple and their attendants, requesting lodging for the night. But they are...*humans*, my king. The Earl and Countess of Oxford."

Alaric pressed his lips together, lest he unleash a roar of frustration. Poor Oliver just looked horrified. Naturally, when the entire castle was in a flurry of preparation for the impending ceremonies, bloody humans would arrive. And he couldn't refuse them lodging, not these two at least. John de Vere, Earl of Oxford, had fought valiantly for the Lancastrians at Bosworth Field and been richly rewarded with several important roles in Henry Tudor's court, including Lord Admiral, Constable of the Tower of London, a seat at the Privy Council, and Lord Great Chamberlain of England. His wife was no less illustrious; Margaret Neville had been sister to the Earl of Warwick, known to humans as the Kingmaker, and aunt to the previous Queen of England, Anne Neville.

"Tell Larkin to prepare a chamber," said Alaric, unable to suppress a sigh. "A fine one. Everyone must behave— these are important humans, great favorites of Henry Tudor, and I need no added tensions right now. Also, ensure Princess Evaine and Queen Siân are aware."

Oliver bowed. "At once, my king. Interesting, is it not, that the earl and countess should travel so far out of their way to call upon you, and so soon after your pledge at Eltham."

"Very, very interesting. Oh, and Oliver..."

"Put away the gold?" said the steward, his lips twitching.

"Yes. Also the best tapestries and anything jewel-encrusted," confirmed Alaric. "Lock the door to Leto's shrine, tell the armorers to conceal their wares, and warn the guards to make themselves scarce for the evening. Anything that makes Blackstone Castle appear more than the remote fortress of a prosperous human knight. Er...new *duke*. And everyone *must* stay in human form."

After Oliver had dashed away to alert the household and the guard was dispatched to open the portcullis and admit the humans, Alaric marched over to the library window to watch the proceedings below. Not for a moment did he believe the earl and countess were here on a friendly or impromptu visit. With all Lord Oxford's new appointments, he had no reason whatsoever to pass through the Welsh Marches, especially to a remote castle in winter. No, these lofty humans certainly had a purpose.

It was just a matter of discovering what that purpose was; and hoping that no one inadvertently revealed that every other soul at Blackstone Castle was a wolf.

Leto help them all.

———

Human guests. Blackstone Castle had *human* guests.

Evaine exchanged an uneasy glance with Siân as the queen's ladies bustled around them, lacing gown sleeves, brushing and plaiting hair, and fastening jewelry in preparation for the impromptu banquet.

Each wolf king's castle was deliberately remote, well away from main roads and constructed to look bleak and uninviting from the outside, so any stray humans *weren't* tempted to approach. Yet now they had guests, not lost travelers, but aristocrats expecting food and shelter, as they would from their human acquaintances.

Something about this just felt wholly wrong. Wholly *suspicious*.

Then again, perhaps her mind was just playing tricks, seeing shadows and darkness when there were none. In truth, she had no personal experience with aristocratic humans. Back in the Eastern Lands, her father had some dealings with them, but her mother always declined, stating she'd seen and heard quite enough working in a tavern. While Evaine had been in hiding, she'd only ever dared contact with peasants; some had been kind, others awful, but all had lived in fear of those with a title. Unlike wolf kings, who protected their pack and lands and considered ample food, well-made clothing, and sturdy housing the bare minimum, it seemed human lords barely cared if their tenants lived or died. Siân had ruled for the best part of two centuries, though, visiting several human royal courts to pledge fealty. She would know more.

As soon as the ladies finished their work and departed the elder wolf queen's large and lavishly-appointed bedchamber, Evaine cleared her throat. "Do you know anything of these, ah, Oxfords? Are they good people?"

Siân's lips twisted. "I know of the earl and his wife. It is true he has shown bravery and talent as a commander on the battlefield, but his many appointments came only because he happened to be on the winning side at Bosworth Field. In the recent past Lord Oxford has not been so fortunate: attainted for treason, fleeing abroad several times, even imprisonment. He has also engaged in privateering. In my eyes, a true measure of character is how someone treats those who depend on him, not merely his equals or superiors. Oxford's wife and mother suffered greatly for his acts. That is one significant difference between wolf and human: females are respected as leaders and warriors, healers and scholars, not merely tolerated because they birth cubs. Wolves always seek counsel from their mate, and would never, ever leave them to starve or be abused. We stand together until the end."

"Like Mother and Father," whispered Evaine.

"*Exactly* like Hugo and Magdalena," replied Siân, briefly reaching out to cup Evaine's cheek.

"Why do you think the Oxfords have come here? It seems very odd," said Evaine, as she nervously smoothed the square bodice of her favored emerald-green velvet gown and ensured her simple gold girdle lay flat. "I mean, it's winter. The weather is foul, the roads are awful, and most humans are busy celebrating the Twelve Days of Christmas at their estates."

"Precisely. It is very odd. And the Welsh Marches are hardly a direct route anywhere. Let me warn you, my dear, tonight will be an exceedingly strange experience. I know Lord Oxford thinks himself very high and mighty and will behave accordingly. And we'll all have to sit there, knowing we could end his life with a single bite or claw swipe."

Evaine giggled then sobered. "How do you bear it? How does Alaric bear it? I can't even imagine having to pledge sword and service to a human king when they change so often and are so *weak*."

"It is tedious beyond belief," admitted Siân, as she adjusted the veil covering her hair then shook out her silver-embroidered cream velvet skirts. "But the other choice is Hera's wrath. And I've seen the terrible things that can happen...oh dear, listen to me ramble on."

Frowning inwardly, Evaine hesitated. Why did it appear the queen had been about to say something and then changed her mind? How odd. "Have you ever met a *good* titled human?" she asked instead.

Siân brightened. "I have. Edward IV's queen, Elizabeth Woodville, and her mother, Jacquetta of Luxembourg. Those two have certain otherworldly gifts and we had some *very* interesting discussions. Be wary of the new King

Henry's mother, though. In truth, be wary of anyone blindly enamored of the crucifix. They despise anyone who speaks, thinks, or acts differently to them. On many occasions in London I was tempted beyond measure to cull the human herd, but Cyrus usually stayed my hand."

Evaine nodded solemnly. More than once she'd overheard Father saying the same thing about culling. Most wolves refrained; fortunately, there were countless ways for fragile humans to perish, and accidents or rash deeds could easily be concealed. "I will certainly need Alaric's steady hand to stay me. Evaine the Bold sometimes doesn't look before she leaps. On that note, we must go and rescue my poor mate. I believe he was entertaining the Oxfords in the library with mulled wine while we dressed?"

"Yes," said Siân with a sigh. "Even diplomats can have their patience worn cobweb thin."

Arm in arm, Evaine and Siân walked in companionable silence to Alaric's library, the trains of their gowns swishing against the smooth stone floor. It was a little eerie how bare the hallway looked; all the gold and gilt that she barely glanced at now had been removed, along with most of the queen's truly exquisite tapestries depicting wolves at play, hunting, or posing with their cubs.

Gah. Wretched humans.

Just before entering the room, Evaine paused and inhaled deeply of the delectable scent lingering around the door. While she wanted no part in entertaining human aristocrats, the chance to spend time with Alaric was most welcome. Especially in here, the place where they had already created so many lusty and truly magical memories; where their mating marks had risen, confirming their fate and future together. These past three days, where she had seen so little of her king, had been a great trial indeed.

"Alaric," she said joyfully as she burst into the library, hurrying over to where he stood beside his desk. However, before she could throw her arms around his waist or go up on her toes to kiss him thoroughly, her mate very stiffly took her hand and placed a brief kiss upon it.

Twice wretched humans!

"My lady," he replied formally, then looked past her and bowed at Siân. "Lady Mother. May I present the Earl and Countess of Oxford. Lord and Lady Oxford, you might remember my mother, the Lady Siân Beaumont, from court."

Both humans inclined their heads. They were disappointingly unremarkable; of a similar average height, each with dark hair. The earl had the lean build of a soldier, with a scar across his cheek that looked like an old arrow wound. The countess was equally slender, with arched eyebrows that made her look perpetually surprised. However, both were richly dressed: him in a black velvet doublet and hose with a heavy chain of office about his neck and a badge with a blue boar on his chest, and her in a costly gown of deep blue velvet with silver underskirt and sleeves.

"Lady Siân," said the earl crisply. "A pleasure to see you again. How grateful you must be that our generous and esteemed King Henry bestowed such an honor on your son. Duke of Blackstone! Quite the elevation for your family."

The queen exchanged a glance with Evaine before tapping her fingernails together. Somehow Evaine swallowed a belly laugh. No. There would be no claws out this evening.

"Such a shock," Siân demurred.

"And this eager creature is your betrothed?" said Lady Oxford coolly. "I suppose any young lady dreams of being a duchess; no wonder she forgets decorum and runs to greet you, Blackstone. Perhaps you'll teach her restraint and courtly ways. One does not address one's husband so informally, child. Especially a duke. Are you from a small village, perhaps?"

Evaine nearly hissed. "Forgive me," she ground out eventually, as Alaric discreetly rubbed his thumb against her palm, a soothing motion. "I was overcome by tender feelings for my ma...my betrothed."

"Something I shall never grow weary of," said Alaric, his voice caressing her even if his tongue could not. "I am fortunate beyond measure to have found a match surely written in the stars. Allow me to present the Lady Evaine de Wynter."

Lady Oxford tilted her head, her expression warming slightly. "I have heard the name de Wynter! Are your people from over Norfolk way?"

"Yes, my lady."

"Wait," said Lord Oxford, his brows furrowing. "Not kin to Sir Hugo de Wynter? Now he was a decent soldier. Damned decent indeed. Well, until he wed the tavern wench. God's blood, scandal of the year, that was! She must have been a witch, no idea how they were received by anyone of standing. People were laughing behind their backs at court, then her cousin of all people kills them both! Such a tale belongs on stage. Or preached from the pulpits as a warning. The perils of marrying far beneath one's own rank."

Scalding, blinding rage surged through Evaine. This pathetic sewer rat dared to speak ill of her beloved parents? One swipe. One claw swipe was all it would take to spill the innards of both these humans on the library floor. Yes, it would create a terrible mess, but Blanche's lye soap had yet to be defeated by anything.

A low snarl rumbled in her chest, and she actually felt her fingers curl and canines sharpen. Lord Oxford might have enjoyed good fortune in battle until this point, but his luck had just run out. Tonight, this human sack of excrement who thought himself noble would die most horribly at the hand of his sworn enemy...

Princess Evaine de Wynter.

———

Did the Earl of Oxford understand how close he was to having his throat ripped out?

Alaric studied the unwanted visitor like he might study a rat cornered by a barn cat. No, Oxford was still twittering like a foolish little squirrel about Hugo and Magdalena. It was laughable. As though the revered and star-risen King and Queen of the Eastern Lands would have cared one whit what a passel of completely unimportant humans thought of their union. Leto, all-powerful and all-knowing, matched hearts and souls. A mate's position or employment, their past lovers, the heaviness of their purse...none of that mattered.

A heartbeat before Evaine slaughtered the most important human noble in the land, Alaric curled his arm around her waist, yanking her to his side. Then, ignoring the shocked gasps of the humans, he leaned down and kissed her deeply, tangling his tongue with hers until she moaned softly. When he'd had his fill of Evaine's sweet lips, he nuzzled her cheek. "No, sweetheart," he murmured. "You may not decorate my library with the earl's entrails. Not this night, anyway. The guests must leave as they arrived, hale and hearty."

Evaine hissed, but eventually took a deep breath and

relaxed against him. Alaric knew a moment of relief. If she'd killed the earl, the entire party including the countess and attendants would require culling, and so many bodies would be a nuisance to dispose of. Besides, many humans would be aware of the Oxford's destination; with the new dukedom and rumors of goldmines already swirling, Blackstone Castle didn't need any further attention.

His mother smiled brightly, although there was clear disappointment in her eyes at his intervention. Bloodthirsty she-wolf.

"Shall we proceed to the Great Hall, my son?" asked Siân archly. "I find I'm quite famished, and crave a side of rare beef. Fresh, juicy and red."

"That sounds delicious," said Evaine, shooting another deadly glare at the earl. "Although aged meat can also be very tasty."

Lord Oxford bowed, his expression revealing both irritation and disdain before it smoothed away into a polite mask. "It is still Christmastide, the season of goodwill and forgiveness to fellow man. Unseemly behavior is easily forgotten, and my countess and I welcome generous hospitality. Lead on, *Your Grace*."

Alaric gritted his teeth. Between *fellow man* and the condescending reminder of the dukedom, Evie might have to wait her turn with the Oxfords. He had no doubt that Lord Oxford was jealous, but that tone, as though the earl was humoring small children in the nursery, was beyond provoking. Their visitor truly thought himself in the position of power.

Forcibly suppressing his irritation, Alaric linked arms with both Evaine and his mother, and they walked toward the Great Hall, the two humans in tow. Shortly afterward the Oxfords began whispering to each other, and Alaric rolled his eyes at the comments regarding a lack of furniture, liking or disliking carpets and artwork, and coveting certain trinkets. These two were actually *assessing* his holdings; no doubt Alaric would receive further tribute requests from King Henry in due course. Removing so many valuables had indeed been the correct path.

Evaine wrinkled her nose. "Do you think," she said softly, "we should offer quill and parchment for their list-making?"

He grinned. "Better that than their own innards to swallow."

His mate deliberately bumped her hip against him, and Alaric nearly laughed at the unspoken reprimand. He certainly understood the warning, though: if Lord Oxford insulted Hugo and Magdalena again, she wouldn't be stayed by a kiss. In truth, he wouldn't attempt it. If the visitors were that foolish, they deserved whatever happened next, diplomacy be damned.

Evaine leaned closer. "The Oxfords certainly require stronger herbs in their bathing water. I know wagon travel makes it more difficult, but surely human inns could offer much better service."

"Don't remind me," muttered Alaric. "My stomach hurt for days thanks to the fare provided. No wonder humans are often ill."

When they entered the Great Hall, he gazed about with pure pride. Despite the burden of ceremony preparation and no warning of the humans' arrival, the cavernous room looked cozy and welcoming. All four fireplaces were lit, fresh rushes had been scattered about so the hall smelled pleasantly of dried mint and lemon, and a trestle table sat in the center with carpets underfoot and five cushioned chairs. Servants waited to pour ale or wine in the pewter goblets provided, while others were already carrying in trays laden with roasted meat, vegetables, a wheel of cheese, loaf of bread with a pat of butter, honey cakes, and even some almond sweetmeats. Alaric sat at the head of the table, with Evaine to his left, and his mother sitting next to her. The Oxfords would sit to his right.

Lady Oxford glanced around as servants pulled out their chairs, her gaze still assessing. "Well, this looks most adequate. Let's eat."

For the next hour or so, the humans were almost amiable as they ate their fill of roasted beef and mutton, a pottage of carrots, turnips, and leeks thickened with barley, and the bread and cheese. The countess even declared she simply must have the honey cake recipe to give to her own cook.

Then the earl dabbed his mouth with a linen napkin, and sat back in his chair. "Excellent meal, Blackstone, just what is required on a cold winter's night. Even the wine was a surprisingly good vintage. However, now we must discuss business. Normally, I would ask the ladies to retire to the solar, but I don't think their minds too simple for this."

Alaric raised a brow. "I don't think their minds too simple for anything, my lord, but pray continue."

Lord Oxford smiled thinly. "Ah, you prefer plain speaking. I much prefer that myself. Very well, so we have no misunderstanding, there is an issue with your betrothal."

Considering how long Alaric had been a judge and emissary, then King of the Western Lands, it was rather startling that a few words from a human could make him forget all his calm, considered dealings. He'd been wrong to stay Evaine's claws; Lord Oxford's head would look much better displayed on a spike.

"An issue?" he said slowly, lest he snarl the reply. "How so, my lord? Who could possibly take issue with my betrothal?"

Lady Oxford coughed delicately, but her eyes glinted with malice. "Why, His Grace the King."

Siân tilted her head, her gaze chilly. "People in this realm are betrothed every day. Why should my son's ma... er, his choice of bride trouble King Henry?"

"I thought *you* would understand," said Lord Oxford sourly, "but it seems both I, and your son, overestimated your intellect. Blackstone is a duke, his marriage is a matter of state. All betrothals must be approved by King Henry to further his vision for a secure and prosperous realm. Appropriate matches, such as a union between de Vere and Neville. We were shocked, so soon after Blackstone received his honor, that he could so blatantly insult his new king."

Alaric took Evaine's hand, not to halt any action, but to gather his own composure. How many times had he already cursed Henry for this dukedom foolishness? A "gift" he neither wanted nor needed, a "gift" he'd already paid for, yet now came another demand? A human in London thinking he could decide who Alaric Dafydd Beaumont, King of the Western Lands's mate would be?

No. Not in a thousand years.

"Lady Evaine is my betrothed," said Alaric, his voice steely. "And next week, she will be my wife."

"Next *week*?" bellowed the earl. "God's blood, no. If you cease and desist this at once, write letters to the king begging his forgiveness with appropriate compensation, I am certain he would accept it. No one need know of your misstep; His Grace might even offer a far more appropriate match. But a duke *cannot* wed someone with a tavern wench in the family, even if the rest are unexceptional. You'll start a war!"

"Just so I understand," said Evaine crisply, her fingernails tapping on the table, "is wedding the wrong person similar in misstep to being attainted for treason? For that hasn't held you back."

Lord Oxford's eyes bulged and his countess gasped.

"Bold girl!" said Lady Oxford furiously. "I can guess why a swift wedding is required, all that wicked peasant blood had you lifting your gown, and now there's a babe, yes? You're as foul as Magdalena. But unlike her, you'll not trap a husband of means and position. *Noblemen marry at the pleasure of the king.*"

Alaric wasn't entirely sure how it happened, but in the blink of an eye the entire table flew across the Great Hall, scattering food and drink, goblets and spoons and plates in all directions. And he stood, one human's neck gripped in each fist, as they dangled helplessly.

"You dare insult me and my mate in our own castle?" he roared, shaking them both like rag dolls, their little feet kicking, their cheeks bulging, the air alive with choking, gurgling sounds. "The ceremony is next week, as I command. And I care not what title you have or chains you hold, if you slander Evaine or Magdalena again, I'll burn your hearts and return your heads to London in baskets! You're not welcome on Beaumont lands. Nor are any other of Henry's advisors. Do *you* understand, my lord?"

"Y-yes," wheezed Lord Oxford, his face a delightful shade of purple.

Alaric dropped them both to the floor. "Leave. Tonight. If you are here in the morning, you'll be hunted for sport."

Stepping over their shaking, coughing, cringing forms, Alaric offered his arm to Evaine and his mother. They both looked surprised yet amused at his most uncharacteristic show of violence toward humans. In truth, he could scarcely believe it.

By the time the trio departed the hall, Alaric's rage was cooling, but with that came a troubling realization: after telling everyone else to behave, *he* had just escalated the war. He'd not acted as a king or a diplomat...but a mate.

Would he live to regret the choice?

CHAPTER
SIX

E vaine stretched and yawned, then cuddled closer to Alaric's shirt-covered chest. This tiny, unfurnished room above the stables was bitterly cold, poorly lit with just one small torch, and more than a little dusty, but it was the only place in the entire castle that wasn't overrun with guests or servants.

No doubt there were assorted courtiers and pack members gnawing their own paws trying to find Alaric so he could decide this final detail or that final adjustment for today's mating ceremony and her official crowning as Queen of the Western Lands. But a stolen hour at dawn, alone with her mate, had been well worth it. Her whole body was wonderfully relaxed after the glorious release Alaric had brought her with his talented fingers. Now she was ready to face the day.

"Do you think they'll find us soon?" Evaine murmured as she pressed kisses to his neck.

He chuckled and held her tighter. "Alas, I think at least a few of my servants know where we are, including my marshal. Willie has diverted at least ten wolves from entering the stables."

She bit her lip. "Poor Willie. He has enough to think about, organizing our upcoming procession around the Western Lands. In some ways, I wish we could just run away together like the younger humans do."

Alaric leaned back slightly, his gaze intent. "Are you nervous about the ceremonies?"

"Not nervous exactly," said Evaine slowly, her heart twinging. "Of course I don't want to make a mistake with everyone watching, trip over my gown train or jumble my words. But it's more...I'm just sad there are no other de Wynters here. My sire should read from the Book of Lore and take our thumbprints and combined blood drop to recognize the royal union. My mother should plait my hair and tell me all the jaw-dropping details about...well, you know. Biting and knotting. Breeding heat. Pregnancy. And my s-sisters would have challenged you to a swordfight. We'd share spiced ale and exchange gifts. You and my brother would go hunting for the ceremonial stag h-heart..."

Tears burned her eyes and she hastily blinked them back lest Alaric think she was upset about today. It was exciting to finally be joining with her mate and to take her place beside him on the Western throne. It was just...she missed her mother and father and sisters and brother so very much. And on the most formal occasion possible for royal wolves, the absence of anyone from the de Wynter pack would be somberly noted. She didn't want somber. She wanted *joyful*.

"Evie..." said Alaric as he stroked her back and smoothed her heavy robe. "I swear that we'll find Isabel and Cecily and Lucan. They will forever have sanctuary here until Lucan can reclaim the Book of Lore and his throne. I know that Darius and Ranulf pledge the same. If your sisters and brother can make it to a royal castle, they'll be safe. And, just like Apollo and Artemis mercilessly avenged all offenses against our Blessed Leto, we shall brutally punish those who murdered your mother and father and enslaved the de Wynter pack."

Evaine growled. "The hatred I feel for Guy Saville knows no bounds. He will pay. One day."

They sat in companionable silence for another quarter hour or so, then Alaric glanced out the small window. "More wolves are waking. I fear we must return to our chambers and pretend we weren't rolling about on hay bales. Mother will be disappointed we ignored her practical advice," he finished, smiling ruefully as he brushed straw from her sleeve.

"I wonder if that particular detail will make it to Henry in London," Evaine replied tartly as she reluctantly stood. "He heard about us before the ink was even dry."

Alaric went still. "That is exactly what continues to bother me, how swiftly those Hera-spawned Oxfords arrived to scold us for offending their king. How did Henry even find out? No human would know of our plans, or the preparation here. It's too remote."

Her stomach sank at the implications. "Surely a wolf wouldn't dare interfere. Do you think...a pack member or servant wants to stop this ceremony? Perhaps collect the bounty on my head? I know the amount is very large."

He shook his head firmly. "I would hope to the depths of my soul the answer is no. Gold wouldn't be an inducement to anyone at Blackstone Castle. But even with hundreds and hundreds of guests, I have armed guards everywhere. Save my brother kings and their personal attendants, no one is permitted to carry weapons within these walls. Blackstone is your home, Evie. Your sanctuary. By this afternoon, you'll be crowned queen. By tonight...my bonded link mate. Mine in every way."

Evaine shivered at the hot promise in his gaze. Indeed, while Alaric's tongue and fingers were truly magical, she yearned to be joined with him completely, his cock lodged deep inside her, flooding her with seed as he bit her mating mark and unlocked their mind link. "And you'll be mine in every way."

"I will. Now, let us go before the castle runs mad. I'm sure Oliver and Larkin will have lists a mile long."

After pulling their warm cloaks around them, Evaine and Alaric left the stables and crossed the courtyard to the castle. One lingering kiss later, they each returned to their own chamber.

When Evaine pushed open the door to her room, the last time she would ever use it, Siân was waiting for her. The fire had been stoked, several candelabra were lit, and fresh water was heating in a wrought-iron bucket.

The queen's lips twitched. "Straw? Really, my dear? Have I taught you nothing?"

Evaine poked out her tongue as she batted the stray evidence from her sleeve. "I've no idea what you speak of, Mother."

They both froze.

"Beg pardon," said Evaine swiftly. "I'm not sure why I said that."

The queen hesitated, her fingers twisting together. "I would never seek to replace Magdalena. I know you loved her beyond measure, may Leto bless her star-soul. But should you wish a mother figure...someone to ask certain questions of, or tweak Alaric's nose if he is being a right royal arse...I am here."

A giggle bubbled in her chest. "Was King Cyrus ever a right royal arse?"

"He had his moments," said Siân fondly, her gaze faraway. "Especially when he overindulged in wine and snored like a thunderstorm. Or grumbled about wolflings being too loud. Or the time he tried to *help* by changing the den I made before I birthed Alaric."

"Oh dear."

"But none of that ever compared to my worst trial: his mother, Ana-Maria. She was an *Ilustrisima Senora*, over-bearing, rude, and quarrelsome, and never missed a chance to tell me I wasn't nearly good enough for her son and his blue Spanish blood. I swore there and then, if I was blessed with a male cub, I would never behave like that. I wanted to be a friend to my new daughter, not an enemy. I won't tell you how to be queen, Evaine, or insist anything remain my preference, for this will be your castle. But should you seek my counsel or experience, I shall offer it gladly."

"Did you like Theda?" asked Evaine, the words rushing out before she could haul them back in.

The queen's eyes widened briefly, then she shook her head. "No. I was in seclusion, so I missed a lot. But when I met her, I knew in my bones she wasn't my son's mate. Theda treated Alaric horribly. She accepted the crown but *shunned* him. Rejected his touch. They never shared a chamber and rarely shared a bed, even in rutting season. I never thought I would say this about a queen, but no one was saddened at her death. The only comment I kept hearing was regret that Alaric would never sire an heir."

Evaine exhaled slowly. Alaric had spoken freely of Theda, but it was reassuring to hear the same message from another source, to know what felt right was right. She and

Alaric were fated mates and Blackstone Castle was exactly where she was meant to be. As queen. "I did have other questions," she said awkwardly. "Those I might ask a mother..."

Siân grinned, so much like her son it was uncanny, and beckoned her over to sit on the fireside cushions. "A she-wolf's first biting and knotting experience is almost impossible to describe. Pleasure and pain intertwine like a rope. I wasn't sure I could bear it, but kept demanding more, more, more. The release is like a storm wave and a starburst and I screamed myself hoarse. As for your first breeding heat... your body offers clues it is coming, because the day before, you'll feel terrible. Headache, sore limbs, fever, sweats. There'll be tears and snarls and you'll want to hurl your mate off the ramparts. Then the next day...Goddess. The need to rut, all the time, will consume you for an entire week. Eat, drink, rut, sleep a little, then start again. That's all. And do not fret, everyone understands."

Her cheeks burning, Evaine nearly rocked on the cushion at the frankness, but she greatly appreciated not having to coax or drag the information out. While she was certain Alaric would teach her everything, it was lovely to not go in completely unaware. "And, uh...what about cubs? I mean, do you know if you conceive?"

"Oh, you'll know," said Siân with a laugh. "Not long after unknotting, you abruptly change into wolf-form, and stay like that until you deliver. Which is such a blessing. Wolves carry for two months, humans carry for *nine*. Ugh. Imagine that! Now, do you have any other questions, or shall I call for Blanche and my ladies to assist you? The mating ceremony is scheduled for mid-morning, and we need to brush your fur and scrub your claws. After I've removed that straw, hmmm?"

All Evaine could do was grin. "Yes, Mother."

———

"It's time! It's time! It's actually time for your mating ceremony. Well, your *real* mating ceremony. With your real mate."

Alaric raised an eyebrow as Wesley darted about the bedchamber as though his hose was aflame. His squire had been ready for hours, his boots polished, his hair actually combed, preening in his new gold and black livery. The eagerness was almost *endearing*.

"Yes," Alaric replied simply. "A half hour and we'll be standing in front of Leto's shrine."

Wesley halted in front of Alaric's looking glass and bowed. "My queen. My *queen*. All hail Queen Evaine of the Western Lands, long may she reign...oh, this is wonderful. A queen means lots of beautiful females will visit...one day she might have cubs! Do not fret, my king, I will ensure your young know all the important skills such as...coaxing more pork slices from Cook. How to stalk a squirrel. And remove a splinter from their thumb with an embroidery needle. Mother taught me that."

Alaric blinked. The way Wesley's mind bounced from one topic to the next was enough to give anyone a severe headache, but today, nothing could change his mood. It was a momentous and glorious occasion indeed. "I am glad to know they'll have such a dedicated tutor."

His squire halted. "Wait. Cubs must be created first. My king, do you know what to do? I can fetch Father, he sired two litters so I presume he has some knowledge. Then again, perhaps Mother just gave him a list of instructions. Father adores lists."

"I am confident on this matter, yes," replied Alaric, his lips twitching. Wolflings were such a curious mix of mature wolf and cub, and it continued to fascinate him how they swayed between the two.

Wesley sighed, actually looking relieved. "Excellent. Is there anything else you need? I will examine all your garments again before the main ceremony, to ensure they are perfect. But that crown is so heavy, I don't even know how you keep it on your head."

Alaric nodded solemnly. In truth, he wondered himself. He usually wore a plain circlet crown and a doublet badge made of gold and jet. But for formal ceremonies, the Western Crown was hauled out of the heavily-guarded Treasury. It had been fashioned centuries ago to resemble Blackstone Castle, with four points that rose several inches above the base of satin-lined, solid Beaumont gold, affixed with pearls and amethysts. One pigeon egg-sized diamond, surrounded by smaller diamonds, decorated the front. The damned thing was *wretchedly* heavy. Fortunately, he only had to wear it for Evaine's official crowning; during the first ceremony at Leto's shrine both he and Evaine would be in wolf form. This was the private, very personal part of the day, only attended by Darius and Ranulf as witnesses, his mother, and Wesley, for it was protocol for a king's squire to attend all formal events.

Once again, his heart clenched for Evaine. The King and Queen of the Eastern Lands should be here to witness their eldest cub's mating ceremony, not star-risen. Isabel, Cecily and Lucan should be challenging him to prove he was strong and brave and clever enough for their sister—not in hiding, perhaps sick or injured, terrified for their lives.

"Did a search party go out, as normal?" Alaric asked abruptly.

Wesley frowned. "I'm not sure. Perhaps they thought not, due to the ceremonies?"

"Run and tell your sire to dispatch a group. The crowning ceremony won't begin until they return. Perhaps one of the princesses might flee here, hidden among the guests."

His squire brightened. "Concealed in a cart, even! Or if not today, while you are out on progress. When I look out my window to the stars, I often ask Leto to restore Princess Evaine's sisters to her, and her brother to the Eastern throne."

"You and me both," said Alaric gruffly, briefly patting Wesley's shoulder. His squire beamed, then dashed away to find his father.

After discarding his heavy brocade robe, Alaric closed his eyes and changed into wolf form. Even now it took a moment to adjust to the change in height and shape, but when he ran his tongue-tip over his fangs, pure lust jolted through him. This night they would have a task far more important than hunting: sinking into Evaine's mating mark, fusing her to him as he knotted inside her and unlocked their bonded mind link.

Anticipation burned brighter than fire, although if he were brutally honest, nerves fluttered in his stomach. What would it feel like to be fully bonded? To speak to each other without talking? To know Evaine's thoughts, and have her know his? For a diplomat, it was actually disconcerting. His mate would know if he dissembled, told a partial truth, or attempted to hide his emotions. Evaine would know *everything*. He would be utterly vulnerable to her and she would be utterly vulnerable to him.

Alaric huffed out a breath, then indulged in a full-body stretch, his claws digging into the rug as he rolled his shoulders and arched his back. Goddess, that always felt good. Next, he padded over to the looking glass to inspect his fur, his tail, even his ears. Never had cleanliness been so important.

"You're in fine form, my king. I swear," said Wesley, as he bounded back into the room. "And a search party will scour the area. There were countless offers; so many wolves want to be the one who escorts a missing de Wynter princess into the castle as a gift to you and the new queen. The guards nearly fought each other. But can we go to the shrine now? I'm ready to present the offerings!"

He almost sighed; Wesley had made no secret of his role in the private ceremony. "Yes, we'll go to the shrine now. Be humble, lest someone accidentally bloodies your nose."

Wesley sketched a solemn bow, but nothing could extinguish his jaunty pride as he smoothed his livery then led Alaric out of the royal bedchamber. "Make way! Make way for King Alaric! He travels to Leto's shrine to be mated!"

Alaric almost rolled his eyes. And yet how different the ceremony procession felt this time! Going to Theda, there had been no sense of urgency. No excitement. Today, Alaric had to force himself to move slowly down the hallway. To not leap downstairs, but regally acknowledge all the cheering servants and guests who had formed lines to toss sprigs of herbs as a wish for good fortune and fertility. Evaine would receive the same as she was led by his mother.

But why was it taking a thousand years to reach Leto's ground-floor shrine? Damn it, when had his castle grown to twice its size?

Alaric growled under his breath, but at last he stood outside the sacred chamber. The double doors were wide open, the stone floor strewn with flowers, herbs, and gold coins. The arched entrance was draped in satin; green and white for de Wynter, and black and gold for Beaumont, and a beautifully embroidered tapestry depicting their crests hung proudly on the wall. His mother had been busy. Inside the chamber, Darius and Ranulf waited next to Rowan, the longtime soothsayer of Blackstone Castle.

"My son and king," called Siân as she approached from the opposite direction, wearing the traditional plain white linen gown of female attendants. "With a glad heart and a merry step I present Evaine de Wynter, blooded princess of the Eastern Lands and your one true fated mate."

"Come to me, Princess Evaine," intoned Alaric. "Let us give thanks to the revered Goddess for her many blessings."

His breath caught as the small crowd parted and Evaine strolled through, her sleek, elegantly deadly form padding soundlessly across the floor. How could he be so fortunate to have this glorious, passionate, saucy she-wolf for a mate?

"I am yours, King Alaric," said Evaine, her green eyes glowing. "Lead me unto Leto."

As they approached the gleaming seven-foot-high marble statue of Leto with the twin flames representing Apollo and Artemis burning brightly, a familiar sense of peace overcame Alaric. Except now there was a warmth and contentment he'd not thought possible. Last time with Theda everything had seemed off; one of the flames had even extinguished and had to be relit!

But not today. Not with Evaine. This was right.

Rowan cleared his throat. Then the kindly soothsayer lifted his arms, his flowing black robes swishing around his ankles. "Beloved Leto, your humble servants King Alaric and Princess Evaine come this day to seal their fated union as decreed by you. In grateful joy, they swear to protect and cherish each other, and bring these offerings to give thanks unto you: the fresh heart of a stag, a flagon of red wine, a bag of gold, and two perfect white blooms."

Smiling proudly, Wesley stepped forward with the items. Darius and Ranulf then carefully arranged them at the foot of the shrine.

Next, his mother curtsied deeply to the statue. "We remember those who have risen to the stars and sit at our revered Goddess's right hand: King Cyrus of the Western Lands; King Hugo of the Eastern Lands; Queen Magdalena of the Eastern Lands. Blessed are their names."

Alaric bowed his head, pressing his paw over Evaine's at her faint sniffle. In truth, it was difficult to hold back his own grief at such profound loss.

"Thank you, Queen Siân," said Rowan, inclining his head. "Now I shall take this needle and draw a blood drop from King Alaric and Princess Evaine to formalize their union."

The sharp pinprick made them both wince, but the soothsayer caught their blood drops on a parchment square and expertly blended them with the needle. Alaric and Evaine pressed their paws to the blood, then together, then onto the parchment once more. Unlike last time, when Theda's soothsayer had snatched the parchment away, a brief blue spark lit up the room, turning the square into unbreakable clear stone and capturing the moment for eternity.

Alaric turned his head. "Greetings, my mate," he rasped unsteadily, quite overcome.

Evaine grinned tearfully. "Greetings, my king."

It was done.

Not even being born a princess had prepared her for the sheer overwhelm of royal mating ceremonies. Or the storm of emotions at being so *alone*.

Evaine closed her eyes and rested her head against the cool stone of the privy chamber wall. She needed a little time for composure; after the private mating ceremony she and Alaric had eaten a small but sumptuous meal with Siân, King Darius and King Ranulf. Although very different to Alaric; Darius so battle-hungry and frightening to behold, and Ranulf so scholarly and sharply amusing, both wolf kings treated her like a cherished sister.

However, once again, the lack of any other de Wynters had scratched her soul. Having someone, anyone to share a memory with, not about the rest of England just the Eastern Lands. The particular scent of the frigid, raging North Sea spray. The feel of newly shorn wool from the staggering number of sheep. Nibbling on freshwater fish plucked straight from the River Yare. Watching Father trade with merchant ships from the Low Countries in all manner of languages. The way certain winds shrieked around the turrets of Ashcross Castle like Hera in a temper...

Where were Isabel and Cecily and Lucan? WHERE?

Evaine gulped in several breaths and dashed a hand across her eyes lest she start sobbing. The Queen of the Western Lands would never display reddened eyes and tear-stained cheeks at a formal occasion. Especially the celebration of a mating that brought her immeasurable happiness.

A soft tap sounded at the privy door. "Evaine? May I come in?"

She stumbled over, her legs still a little unsteady after changing back to human form, and pulled the door open to smile at Siân. "I'm quite well and ready to dress for my crowning."

Siân nodded, clear sympathy in her gaze. "I understand needing a moment, my dear. Do you know how many times today I've turned to Cyrus and he's not there? I am so glad you met my mate, even if you were just a cub. Cyrus would simply adore you now. But it is very, very difficult when a joyful time also reminds us of great sadness. Or great anger."

Stepping forward, Evaine clasped the elder queen in a tight hug. "Thank you. For your welcome. Your kindness. Your humor. And Alaric, of course."

"Ha! Of course! Now, let us get you crowned. I'm afraid the garment layers and jewels are many, it is a miracle a Western Queen can move at all."

Evaine laughed, but two hours later she wasn't nearly so amused. Perhaps outside in the cold January air it would be better, but in a ground-floor dressing chamber with a well-stoked fire blazing and ten attendants darting about, it felt like she might suffocate. First, she'd been sponged with herbed water and dried with soft towels. Then, after being dressed in a whisper-thin embroidered linen shift and silk stockings fastened by satin garters, came a cream velvet kirtle that tied at her waist. Next was a heavy gold brocade gown trimmed with diamonds and pearls that actually required several attendants to lift over Evaine's head due to the weight and voluminous train. Siân had then laced on Evaine's cream-and-gold sleeves, lined with satin and ermine for warmth, and fastened a solid gold and jet girdle around her waist.

Evaine almost swayed as she peered at the looking glass in front of her, but alas, there was more to come. Bejeweled rings for her fingers, wide gold bracelets for her wrists, and a sturdy gold necklace set with twelve diamonds the size of her thumbnail. Her hair was brushed to a crackling shine, then plaited and coiled at her nape, secured with gold pins and a short sheer gold veil. "Oh my."

"I know," said Siân, grimacing. "And there's still the queen's crown to come. Fortunately, you only have to wear that on the dais."

"How do I walk to the courtyard?" asked Evaine, only half-jesting. A fully laden carriage would weigh less than this gown and gold.

"Very slowly."

It took a full half-hour to walk from the dressing chamber to the spacious courtyard; by the time Evaine reached the thick crimson carpet near the foot of the dais, sweat dripped down her back, even in the crisp, cold winter air. Goddess! The crowd! There must be thousands of wolves dressed in their best clothes, crammed into the space. While most stood, some were seated on tiered wooden benches, others lined the ramparts, while more still leaned out windows or were perched on the roofs of various outbuildings. Darius and Ranulf sat on cushioned chairs to the rear of the dais, their guards kneeling around them.

But finally Evaine's gaze reached Alaric on his throne, equally bejeweled, gilded and miserable in his majestic attire, and her mood improved. They were in this together.

A trumpet flourish sounded and a herald stepped forward. "Hear ye! Hear ye! The union of King Alaric of the Western Lands and Princess Evaine of the Eastern Lands has been decreed and blessed by Leto herself. May it now be known to all: Evaine is queen, long may she reign."

"*Evaine is queen, long may she reign!*" echoed the crowd.

Alaric rose to his feet and held out a hand. "Come and be recognized, Queen Evaine."

With the assistance of Siân, the attendants, and Rowan the soothsayer, Evaine was discreetly hauled up four steps to the stage and escorted to Alaric's side. When he took her hand and rubbed his thumb over her knuckles, she reveled in the reassuring touch.

Two armed guards carried in the queen's crown, an elaborate, only slightly smaller version of the king's, except it was entirely covered in diamonds and pearls and lined with gold velvet. Rowan took the crown and lifted it high. "To the North! Queen Evaine of the Western Lands. To the South! Queen Evaine of the Western Lands. To the East! Queen Evaine of the Western Lands. Evaine is queen, long may she reign."

"*Evaine is queen, long may she reign,*" bellowed the crowd.

The soothsayer then placed the startlingly heavy crown upon Evaine's head and offered an ancient blessing before he turned to the crowd, his arms outstretched. "Wolves of the Western Lands, greet your anointed ruler King Alaric and his true mate Queen Evaine."

The cheers and applause were deafening. Alaric smiled and lifted their clasped hands, before turning, very slowly, to acknowledge his subjects.

Alaric squeezed her hand. "Not long to go now. I'm so very proud of you," he murmured.

About to reply something saucy, Evaine instead froze as her gaze settled upon a cloaked figure standing on the stone ramparts. A tall, plump female who at first glance appeared to be an elder wolf, with a walking stick, lined face and silver hair. Until their gazes locked...and the she-wolf blew her a kiss and traced a heart in the air.

Evaine gasped. Only one female she knew had ever done that. A beautiful ray of sunshine who raided the kitchens for honey cakes, loved to dance, and could always be depended upon to provide a reassuring hug or kind word when anyone was sad or scared. *Someone so reluctant to leave a warm bed or cushion in front of the fireplace that she would blow a kiss and trace a heart rather than get up.*

ISABEL.

A cry tore from Evaine's throat and she staggered forward, intending to run. Naturally, her ceremonial garments prevented that entirely, and she barely kept the queen's crown atop her head as she wobbled in place on the dais. Wretched train! Wretched jewels!

Alaric moved closer. "Sweetheart? Do you feel faint?"

"No," she replied breathlessly, looking frantically along the ramparts for her sister. But the cloaked figure had vanished. "I thought...I thought I saw..."

Her voice trailed off as doubts crept in. It had been ten long years; all she remembered was her sister as a cub. Just because Isabel had been plump then didn't mean anything now, especially if she had gone without food on many occasions. As for blowing a kiss and tracing a heart, perhaps many did that. Besides, the female had been easily fifty feet away. Too far to see her eye color, or examine her ankle for the small crescent-shaped mark Isabel had since birth.

No, seeing her sister was wishful thinking. Evaine had wanted another de Wynter to be present so badly for her crowning she'd conjured something that simply wasn't real. The time had come to accept that she might never see her sisters and brother again.

"Saw what?" asked Alaric, his low tone more urgent. "A mercenary? Concealed weapons?"

Evaine sighed. "Nothing like that. It's foolish, really. I

thought I saw Isabel, but I was wrong. It was just some poor elder wolf wishing us well."

Her mate hesitated. "Are you sure? It would make sense if your sister was in disguise. I can send out another search party. With a signed note from you, so Isabel knows she has sanctuary here."

"No," she said firmly. "The female wore a long cloak and had silver hair, and was gone in the blink of an eye. To be honest, with this anvil crown crushing my head, I'm surprised I'm not seeing fairies and unicorns."

Alaric smiled ruefully as he waved to a group of wolves who were toasting them with tankards of ale. "The sooner these crowns are back in the Treasury, the better. I'm sure my skull has a gold imprint. But we can leave the dais at any time, all the official parts are complete...my queen."

Evaine whimpered softly as fierce desire coursed through her body. "Not *all*."

A slow smile curled Alaric's lips and his eyes glittered. "Then let us retire and attend to the remaining matter most thoroughly."

She inclined her head. "Yes, my king."

CHAPTER

SEVEN

A ll Alaric wanted to do was take Evaine to bed. But of
course, there was a bloody damned ceremony for
that as well.

"You are doing well, brother. I'd have personally hurled
every single courtier into the moat by now," muttered
Darius as they followed Rowan up the narrow spiral staircase toward the king's bedchamber.

Alaric smiled grimly at the thought. Today, the endless
protocols and procedures, having to remain even-tempered
at all times, answering questions, and engaging in inane
chatter with guests and dignitaries was requiring a truly
Herculean effort. "I am about a tail twitch away from doing
just that. I don't recall everything taking this long last time,
or being this tedious."

The King of the Southern Lands snorted as he impatiently rapped his fingers against his ceremonial sword hilt.
Usually Darius wore nothing but black, but for formal occasions such as this, he deigned to wear the Southern colors.
In truth, an embroidered ruby-red doublet and silver hose
never made him appear any less terrifying or battle-ready.

"Ah, but you weren't cross-eyed with lust for Theda. I see the way you gaze at Evaine. You burn for her...and something more as well."

Alaric harrumphed. "Have you considered searching for your own mate instead of watching me and mine?"

"Death has no mate," growled Darius, his face shuttering as they continued down a brightly candlelit hallway. "But let me know if you require assistance in removing courtiers, *Your Grace*. I'm in the mood to spill blood."

"There is no need to twist the dagger, brother," said Alaric. "As for spilling blood, you are always in the mood to do that. It's why you are feared across the realm. Our colors really are suitable for our thrones; mine dipped in gold, yours dipped in the blood of your enemies."

"Indeed," agreed the other king, although he didn't smile. Instead an odd expression settled across his scarred countenance. "Even more so today."

"Why?" Alaric asked curiously, eager for distraction until he could be alone with Evaine and discard the glittering mountain range currently crushing his skull. The urge to change to wolf form and claw his ceremony finery to shreds was becoming unbearable. "Did something happen? An insult, perhaps? I find it hard to believe anyone would dare. You aren't known for temperance."

Darius actually hesitated, which was more than a little alarming. Why such reluctance? "You are correct, brother— no insult occurred. In truth, I wonder if I'm suffering from too much fresh air. My mind is always clear amid the sweet stench of the River Thames and London, but today I've been on edge. It's as though...I don't know, like I nearly had something very important in my grasp but lost it. The feeling came over me while we were in the courtyard for your queen's crowning and now I cannot purge it from my mind. I had a similar feeling each time I fought Guy Saville on de Wynter land. There is some connection, but I don't know what it is and I fear I will run mad."

Alaric blinked. Never had Darius sounded so unsure. Or confused. He was the warrior who studied his enemies and exploited every weakness, who charged into the fray and defeated his foes with courage and skill and steely determination. "What if..." he began cautiously, "what if Leto is not in fact angry at you and is instead guiding you toward your fated mate?"

His brother king scowled blackly. "Of course she is angry. The Blessed Goddess gifted me one talent. *One*. And that is warfare. Yet I have repeatedly failed her, and the de Wynters, in taking back the Eastern Lands and Book of Lore from the usurper. Besides, no female would survive a king who revels in darkness and destruction. So I'll keep studying Guy Saville until I know him better than he knows himself. I'll torment his followers until they abandon him, then unleash a vengeance so terrible even Hades would be impressed. The matter of she-wolves and cubs, I'll leave to you and Ranulf. The Northern King is doing a sterling job, escorting your mother."

The abrupt change in topic was almost Wesley-like, but Alaric didn't press the issue. It wouldn't matter what he said, Darius was resolute in his belief of Leto's fury with him. The only she-wolves he entertained were strictly for one night, and he mostly shunned anyone other than his brother kings or his commanders. The Southern Lands might be very safe, but there was little merriment or joy. All the spoils of war went into weapons, even cubs were trained to fight rather than play.

In any event, after walking for an eternity, the procession finally reached the king's bedchamber. Once again

Alaric had a role to play, but Leto willing, Evaine waited inside. Goddess, he needed her. Just them, alone and naked.

Rowan banged his ceremonial staff three times on the bedchamber door. "The King is here! Is all in readiness?"

Moments later, the door swung open to reveal two lines of female attendants dressed in their plain white linen gowns, on either side of the entrance. In the doorway, Wesley bowed low. "Greetings, my king. Evaine is queen, long may she reign. Your fated mate awaits you."

Alaric nodded, gritting his teeth against the over-whelming desire to simply roar *LEAVE*. Instead, he followed the soothsayer into the chamber, watching impatiently as the elder wolf scattered drops of blessed oil around the room, and placed two sprigs of herbs upon each pillow. Then Evaine emerged from the small adjoining room wearing a heavy gold velvet robe, her blond hair unbound and gleaming down her back. She winked at him before demurely curtsying. "My king."

Goddess. The heady scent of her! And was she naked under that robe? He wanted to tear the garment from her beautiful body and feast on her sweet cunt until she screamed herself hoarse. Just one of the many, many things he would do to her this night...

Lust surged through him and a low growl rumbled in his chest. Evaine visibly trembled, her nipples peaking against the fabric of the robe, and that was enough to change his mind about enduring protocol.

"Thank you," Alaric said to the small crowd of wolves behind him, his tone polite but uncompromising. "That will be all."

Darius and Ranulf both smirked as they inclined their heads, but departed immediately. His mother offered a jaunty wave, then practically dragged Wesley from the chamber. Rowan just looked perplexed that he wouldn't be reading his prepared speech, lighting all twenty ceremonial candles, burning incense in the fireplace, and directing the lifting and carrying of Alaric and Evaine to bed. Fortunately, apart from some hand-wringing, the soothsayer merely sighed and bowed, gesturing for the ten attendants to follow him from the room.

At last, Alaric was alone with his crowned queen. His true fated mate. Should he say something? Make a declaration to recognize the importance of such an occasion?

Alaric opened his mouth but Evaine untied the sash at her waist, the velvet robe fell to the floor, and the words departed his mind.

"Goddess," he breathed instead, drinking in her naked form like a parched wolf at a clear mountain stream. "You are the most beautiful creature on this earth, my queen."

Evaine sauntered forward, her hips swaying and breasts bouncing. "And you," she purred, "are one very overdressed king. Let me be your squire."

His mate then proceeded to torment him.

After carefully removing his heavy crown and returning it to a velvet-lined wooden chest, Evaine went up on her toes to run her fingers through his hair, lightly scratching and firmly pressing until he groaned at the soothingly sensual touch. Then, with great concentration, she slowly, so damned slowly, unfastened the diamond buttons on his gold and black doublet and unlaced it from his black hose.

"Just tear them off," he growled as he ran his hands over her silken flesh, cupping her breasts and thumbing the pretty pink peaks.

Evaine gasped as though shocked, but her green eyes gleamed with mischief. "I could never treat such lovely and expensive fabric so carelessly," she murmured as she removed the garments and laid both over the chaise near the enormous four-poster bed.

"You don't fool me, Evie," Alaric replied, shameless in his attempts to break her resolve. "Your nipples are harder than diamonds and I'm drowning in the delicious scent of your soaked cunt. I know you need my mouth. My fingers. My cock. To scream with pleasure, over and over."

His mate almost faltered, her fingernails briefly scraping his linen shirt like she might claw it off. Unfortunately, Evaine then regained her composure and grasped the hem of his shirt to lift over his head and Alaric groaned at the too-light touch when he needed her claws raking his skin. But at last he stood equally naked before her, and pure male pride burned through him as her gaze caught on his rapidly hardening cock.

Smiling, he took his shaft in hand, gripping and squeezing the thick length as she avidly watched. "See something you want, my queen?"

Evaine pressed her thighs together. "Can I take your cock in my mouth? Suck it until you spend?"

Goddess. He wanted that more than anything, but had to deny her. And he *hated* denying her.

"Not this night, sweetheart," Alaric replied softly. "You'll take every drop of seed I have in that hot little cunt when I knot. And bite your mark."

She whimpered. "Is it time? I need that. I need it so badly."

"I know," Alaric replied, tenderly cupping her cheek. "And yes, it's time. But first I must prepare you. Go and wait for your mate in bed. For soon and forevermore, it will be *our* bed."

Evaine stared at him, her eyes glittering with fierce

need. With lust. Then she curtsied. "As you command, my king."

———

On such a long day of traditional pomp and ceremony, it had seemed like they would never reach this moment. But here they were, together and alone.

Princess Evaine de Wynter was now Evaine Beaumont, Queen of the Western Lands. And in this lavish bedchamber she would discover all the secrets of the mating bed: the knotting, the biting, and the bonded mind link that would result. As Siân had said, how pleasure and pain could intertwine like a rope.

Evaine bit her lip as anticipation, excitement and nerves coiled together in her belly. Then, straightening her shoulders, she climbed up onto the enormous oak four-poster bed. With heavy black velvet curtains that could be drawn, it was like a small room and exquisitely beautiful: the wood intricately carved and sporting the Beaumont crest, the tester mattress firm and comfortable, and linen sheets so fine they felt like cool water beneath her hands and knees. Helpfully, the servants had turned back the thick quilt so she didn't have to wrestle with it. All she had to do was lie back on a small mountain of soft pillows...and wait for her king.

"Is the bed to your liking?" asked Alaric, as he opened a small locked chest and rummaged within it.

"Not quite," Evaine replied. "You are so far away."

A small smile curved his lips. "My queen requires a distraction. Touch yourself while I gather what's needed."

Her brow furrowed. "What's *needed*? Surely only your cock and my sheath?"

Alaric laughed. "Eventually, sweetheart. Now do as your king commanded."

Oh, this was to be the way of it? He would order and she would obey? Perhaps this king had forgotten he was mated to a de Wynter. Ha. Alaric Beaumont had lessons to learn.

Closing her eyes, Evaine lounged against the pillows, then slid her hands up to cup her breasts, teasing her jutting nipples with her thumbs. Oh yes, that felt good. Next, she pinched the tender peaks, unable to suppress a low whimper at the jolt that arrowed straight to her heated core. Lifting her eyelids the barest slit, she peeked at her mate, who was *definitely* watching her little show.

This time she pinched her nipples as Alaric would, with a firm tweak. A gasp of delight tore from her throat, and she was rewarded with one of his low growls, the sort that immediately coaxed a trickle of honey from her needy channel. She had nearly distracted him from whatever he was fetching, but not quite.

Smiling inwardly, Evaine allowed one hand to trail down over her ribs and belly until it hovered just over her mound. Then she began lazily stroking her bush, before daringly parting the crisp hair to circle her throbbing pleasure bud.

"Mmmmm," she moaned as she delved down further to wet her fingertips in her own honey before returning to rub a little harder. "Oh, yesssss..."

Without warning, her hand was yanked away, and Evaine's eyes flew open to see her mate standing beside the bed, looming over her.

"Once more I see," Alaric rasped, as he licked the honey from her fingers, "my queen is both lusty and wicked."

Evaine fluttered her lashes innocently. "Whatever do you mean? I merely obeyed your instructions, my king."

He growled again, and her core throbbed mercilessly. How in Leto's name did he *do* that?

When Alaric settled on the bed beside her, she brazenly spread her thighs and tilted her hips, fully expecting him to feast as promised. Instead, he held up a leather drawstring bag, then tipped the contents between her legs. "Preparation."

Evaine's eyes widened. There were three cock-shaped objects: two made of polished stone, one about the size of her mate's huge shaft and the other smaller. The third cock appeared to be solid gold, about the size of Alaric's thumb. Each had a smooth metal ring at the top, and there was also a small vial of oil. "What do you mean to do with those?"

Briefly, his gaze turned serious. "I'm not sure how much you've been told...did Mother offer detailed answers?"

"I know some things," said Evaine. "Such as what goes where. And that the sensation is...a lot. Pleasure and pain intertwined like a rope, Siân said."

Alaric nodded. "It *is* a lot. And remember, in this part I don't have a great deal more experience than you. Theda... did not want this with me. And we were never mind-linked because her mating mark was false."

"Well, I want this more than anything," blurted Evaine, restless on the bed. "And if you don't move faster, I'll...I'll..."

"You'll what?" he asked lazily, before bending his head to lash her nipple with his tongue.

She cried out and arched her back, desperate for the rough suckling she preferred. But her mate continued to torment her aching nipples with gentle laps and soft kisses until she wanted to scream not in ecstasy, but in pure frustration. It felt good, but it wasn't nearly enough. "*Alaric.*"

"What do you need, sweetheart?"

Evaine glared at him. "Your cock. At once. *Your queen demands it.*"

Alaric sucked in a breath. "Do you know how hard that makes me, hearing those words? Having a mate who craves me?"

Her heart twinged at the reminder, how that evil imposter had devastated her mate with such treachery. Such *betrayal*. It was one thing to tell Alaric how much she wanted him, but far better to show him.

Turning onto her side, Evaine cupped his cheek and leaned forward to press kisses all over his face, his neck, his throat. Then she licked his lips, before nipping his bottom lip, sharply, a she-wolf marking her territory. "As I said in the library, Alaric. You. Are. *Mine.*"

In the blink of an eye she lay flat on her back, her mate's mouth engulfing her nipple. All Evaine could do was tangle her fingers in his hair and moan as he suckled her with such glorious hunger. Yet when his hand cupped her mound, his middle finger penetrating her deeply as his thumb rubbed her pleasure bud, she writhed and spent with a wild cry.

However, Alaric was nowhere near done with her preparation. Next, he reached for the smaller polished stone cock, his gaze never leaving hers as he trailed the smooth end over the heated skin of her inner thigh. "I know you need to be filled, Evie. But I don't want to hurt you. With the knotting...my cock and your cunt will swell, locking us together for perhaps a half hour. This provides the best chance of conception, although that can only happen if you're in your breeding heat. Starting with the dildos will ease you into being stretched and stuffed full. I'll wet this one with your own juices first."

Evaine swallowed hard, both loving the frank, open conversation and loathing the delay to further pleasure.

Siân had spoken of storms and starbursts! "Why not the smallest, er, dildo? The gold one?"

His golden gaze darkened, and she quivered at the lusty promise there. "Because, my queen, that one is for your arse."

She gasped, both shocked and fascinated at the thought. "Then do it. Hurry. *Hurry*."

"Oh no. We have all night."

For what seemed like hours, Alaric teased her drenched center with the stone dildo until it was glistening wet with honey. Then, slowly and carefully, he began pressing it inside her.

Evaine whimpered at the onslaught of so many new sensations. The cool, sleek, yet unyielding stone as it glided against her hot inner walls. The slight sting as her untouched channel expanded to admit the invader. But most compelling: the throbbing ache that insisted upon movement. And not this careful gentleness, but something raw and untamed. "More," she begged. "Faster. Harder. *Something*."

"Very well," said her conqueror benevolently, as he withdrew the dildo then pushed it back in, setting up a delicious advance and retreat that made her entire body hum. Not long now. Something wonderful was building and building...ohhh yes, just a little more...

Without warning, he removed the stone dildo entirely and set it aside.

Evaine hissed and flashed her fangs. "No! Why did you stop?"

"Because you need to be fully prepared for knotting. The pain that will come with the pleasure," said Alaric, his words calm, but his gaze intense. "That dildo was just a sample, now comes the first course. It might be easier if you tilt your hips and bring your knees to your chest."

After coating the large stone cock in a little oil, he nudged her entrance. Evaine gulped at the size increase, actually panting as her mate slowly but relentlessly eased the dildo into her channel. It was too big! She rocked her hips, groaning as that assisted the stone shaft to sink deeper.

"You are doing beautifully," Alaric praised, leaning down to kiss her shoulder as he alternated twisting the dildo inside her and moving it in and out. "Now I'm going to add the gold one to your arse."

Goddess. The dildo might have looked small, but it felt *enormous* as it penetrated her tight back entrance. And so very strange! The metal was even colder than the stone and her anus strongly resisted the solid object before seeming to suck it in, her inner walls melting around it.

"Alaric," she stuttered, her fingernails digging into her knees as the burning stretch and aching fullness danced on the edge of pain. Could she do this? Her mind said no, but the way her pleasure bud throbbed suggested something else entirely. "Do something...touch me."

Moments later, Alaric began moving both dildos, sometimes together, sometimes separately, and Evaine bucked, her head thrashing on the pillow as once again that wave built and built and she thought she might go mad without release. Then he nudged her pleasure bud and she screamed, her head falling back as ecstasy crashed upon her.

Storms and starbursts indeed...and there was still so much more to come.

———

Nothing gave Alaric greater satisfaction than making his queen, his true fated mate scream with pleasure.

Evie was so lusty, so eager to learn. If his cock didn't hurt so much to be inside her, if his fangs weren't aching to sink into her mating mark, he could have done this for hours. She was so damned beautiful. And the scent of her need, of her readiness to be plundered...he would happily drown in it.

"Alaric," Evaine whispered unsteadily, her eyes dazed, her skin flushed pink, and her breasts rising and falling as she struggled to catch her breath. "I...ah..."

A certain warmth, a fierce protectiveness curled around his heart. He would do anything for this she-wolf. *Anything.* "Shhh, sweetheart, just rest for a bit," he soothed, as he carefully removed the dildos from her cunt and arse. Both holes gaped a little, swollen and tender and slick with honey, and his head swam with the primitive urge to fill her to overflowing with seed. "I'll pour you some wine."

Taking a deep breath to compose himself, Alaric reached over for the flagon of wine and goblets on a gold tray beside the bed. After pouring for his mate, he watched in satisfaction as she gulped it greedily before lying back on the pillows, a small smile curling her lips. Then he took a sip of his own wine. It was rich and full-bodied, but never could the beverage compare to the taste of Evaine.

Soon, she moved restlessly on the bed, her heels digging into the sheets as she rubbed her arse back and forth. "Have you finished your wine?" Evaine asked impatiently.

He smothered a grin as he set his half-finished goblet down. "Why? Do you need something, my queen? Some honey cakes, perhaps?"

With the nimble grace only a she-wolf could demon-strate, Evaine rolled onto her front. Then his mate sprang up onto her hands and knees, circling her hips and swaying her arse as she spread her thighs wide. "Knot me. Bite me. *Now*."

Almost speechless with lust, Alaric stared hungrily at the banquet laid out before him. Unable to resist, he leaned down, inhaling deeply of her scent. Then he extended his tongue and licked her honey-soaked cunt, one long, slow lap to ensure his mouth tasted nothing else.

She moaned, a needy, pleading sound.

"Hmmm," he mused, as he licked her again, reveling in her breathless cries as his cock hardened to the point of pain. "You do appear ready for me, sweetheart. But how can I be sure?"

"Please, Alaric," Evaine replied, the words seemingly wrenched from her, a true royal female surrendering at last. "Please."

He took his cock in hand, giving it one hard squeeze before rubbing his thumb across the seed-wet head. No stone or solid gold dildo could compare to how hard he was right now. He was ready to rut himself senseless. To spend deep in Evaine until he drained his cock dry.

Pressing tender kisses along his queen's spine, Alaric curved himself over her so his chest was pressed to her back. Then, his heart thundering, he guided the head of his cock to her cunt entrance, coating it in her juices before pushing it in.

She gasped, her inner walls rippling around his length, and he almost spent there and then. Surely nothing in the world could compare to this. "Yes, that's the way, sweetheart. Take all of your king."

"I...I can't," she choked out, bucking a little.

"You can," Alaric replied firmly, nipping her shoulder, and her hot, tight cunt rippled around him again as he continued until he was balls-deep inside her. "Now. Now we rut."

Withdrawing slowly until just the head of his cock was submerged, he thrust back in then did the same again, setting a rhythm that grew increasingly harder and rougher. But Evaine was no passive recipient; his mate's head thrashed, her fingernails clawing at the sheets as she pressed back against him, luring his cock deeper. Indeed, she was actively provoking him to thrust with more force until he slammed into her, the sweet symphony of flesh slapping flesh and sensual grunts and pants echoing in the bedchamber.

"Bite me," Evaine snarled, her hips churning. "*Bite me.*"

A low growl rumbled in his chest. Alaric slid one hand under her, briefly pausing to pinch her nipples, before encircling her throat to hold her in place. His queen's mating mark seemed to glow, the crown and two stars clearly illuminated even in soft candlelight.

Rutting her brutally, relentlessly now, his cock as deep inside her cunt as it could possibly go, Alaric swiped his tongue across Evaine's mating mark. Sweetness filled his mouth, even sweeter than her honey. Mindless with need, his fangs elongated and with a feral roar he sank them into the back of her neck.

Evaine screamed, her cunt clamping around him like a vise as she spent, and just like at their mating ceremony, a flash of blue light lit up the chamber. His cock swelled, impossibly large, and Alaric roared again as they locked together, the pleasure so intense it was painful. Then his seed released, gushing and gushing inside Evaine like a damned waterfall, like he'd never spent before in his whole bloody life, and it was so perfect he could only say her name over and over like a chant: "Evie. *Evie.*"

Eventually they collapsed onto the bed in exhaustion, but somehow Alaric summoned the strength to roll them onto their sides so he didn't crush Evaine with his bulk. Then he carefully, gently, withdrew his fangs from her mating mark and lapped at the trickle of blood on her silken skin, sealing the small wound closed. In moments, it began healing.

Evaine made a humming sound, pulling his arm tighter around her. "I understand now why Siân said that was indescribable. There isn't a word for that level of pleasure. Storms and starbursts don't even begin to explain it."

Alaric kissed her shoulder, then reached for the sheets and quilt to pull over them both. Even with a fire blazing in the hearth, and after such vigorous activity, their bodies would soon cool. "Are you well? Not too sore?"

She giggled. "I do feel a bit tender down there, but it's not like you can fetch a hot cloth, is it?"

He couldn't halt an answering chuckle. "No, not for a while. I'm afraid there is no such thing as a swift wolf coupling. Not cock in cunt, anyway."

"I don't mind. It's not like I can move. I no longer have bones, only flesh and blood," said Evaine, nestling against his chest until every inch of her was pressed against him.

"Then rest, sweetheart," Alaric murmured, his eyelids getting heavier. It wouldn't hurt to indulge in a little slumber.

It might have been minutes or hours later, it was difficult to tell when both the fire and candles still burned brightly in his bedchamber, but to his great relief, his cock had softened and slipped free of Evaine. What had woken him?

Then Alaric heard a sound, like faint windchimes.

However, when he sat up and peered around the room, there was nothing amiss.

Shaking his head, he lay back down and closed his eyes.

"No, don't go back to sleep, Alaric. It's about time that tongue went to work again."

Alaric grinned. "So demanding, my queen. Perhaps your tongue should go to work instead."

Evaine yelped. "What?"

His eyes flew open, his brow furrowing in confusion. "Why that sound? You started the conversation."

"I didn't say a word!" she retorted, her eyes wide.

Alaric sighed. "You plain as day said, 'No, don't go back to sleep, Alaric. It's about time that tongue went to work again.' I'm unsure why, after this night, you yelped like a human virgin."

Her cheeks went a very becoming shade of pink. "I didn't say that," she whispered. "I *thought* it."

He went very still. "Just before, I thought I heard wind-chimes. I wonder if that is how the bonded mind-link begins. Think of something else."

"Very well."

Alaric waited. And waited. "Are you thinking something?"

"Yes," Evaine replied, looking a little disappointed.

He grimaced. "Perhaps it takes a while. I honestly don't know how it happens, whether it's a sudden gift or if it gradually grows stronger. I can ask Mother in the morning. Are you hungry? Would you like some honey cakes?"

"An entire plateful, if possible," his mate said with a rueful smile.

"Your wish is my command," Alaric replied as he climbed out of bed and offered an elaborate bow. Then he sauntered to the small table in front of the fireplace and leaned over to pick up a plate of freshly baked cakes and a small pat of butter.

"That is such a fine arse. Perhaps I could nibble on that instead."

He laughed. "After we've had our fill of honey cakes, you are more than welcome to do so."

Evaine made that yelping sound again. "Argh! Why do you only hear *those* thoughts?"

"Because you want me to hear them, my queen."

She gasped, her whole face lighting up, and it was like the sun breaking through a cloud. "I heard that!"

Relief once again swept through him. Much like Evaine, he hated not knowing things, and to be unable to offer comfort or instruction was unendurable. But in all honesty, he wouldn't be terribly aggrieved if she couldn't hear *everything*. Opening his heart and mind when it had been closed so long was a mammoth task. "It seems to work best when we're not trying to force it," Alaric said cautiously, as he returned to the bed with the honey cakes.

She smiled brightly. "Then let us eat. After that, well..."

Alaric inclined his head as his cock began to harden. Some things required no words, bonded mind link or not.

CHAPTER
EIGHT

"A s you can see, the carts are nearly fully loaded, my queen. Are you sure there is nothing I can add to make your travel more comfortable? Even a particular trinket or pillow?"

As the cold, misty dawn air swirled around the torches lighting up the courtyard, Evaine smiled and shook her head at Willie, the castle marshal. She couldn't fault his attention to detail, or any of the plans he had made for the impending month-long progress to introduce her to Alaric's subjects. The marshal had consulted her continuously on preferences for lodging and food and audiences, even inconsequential things like musical instruments to be played at entertainments or her favorite flowers. At no time had she felt like a piece on a chessboard, forever waiting to be moved this way or that. But now all the castle guests had departed, and the sketches for her and Alaric's official portrait were complete. It was time to leave the sanctuary of Blackstone Castle.

"No," said Evaine. "I am more than content. I don't

really have anything in the way of personal trinkets...well, none at all, actually."

Willie winced and kicked at a small stone with the toe of his boot. "Ah, forgive me. I didn't mean to make you sad."

"You didn't," she hastily assured him, wanting to wince herself at the ill-thought comment. As a crowned queen, she needed to be far more mindful around servants. Far more discreet.

In truth, she was struggling to calm her inner nerves about the journey they were about to commence. The prospect remained daunting in so many ways beyond the obvious change that she was now queen. After ten years running from town to town and village to village, it was hard to be excited about a royal progress that had no less than twenty stops. *Twenty*! And they would be traveling over 700 miles, in the middle of winter, for it was custom in Wolfdom to introduce a new queen to her subjects as soon as possible, rather than waiting for summer as the humans did.

Really, she felt rather foolish for not knowing just how vast Alaric's kingdom was. While it encompassed the entire principality of Wales, it also stretched north to Hadrian's Wall, as far east as Derby, and as far south as Cirencester. Although both Willie and Captain Bardolf had assured her she would have warriors dedicated to her safety, and that the king's personal guard of fifty highly trained and heavily armed warriors would accompany them the entire way... the second half of the journey alarmed her most. On several occasions they would be close to the Eastern Lands border.

What if they were set upon by a large pack of mercenaries? Or Guy Saville himself? There were plenty of places where a traveling party could be ambushed.

Evaine shuddered. As Queen of the Western Lands,

some might claim she was no longer a threat or easy target, and the usurper would leave her alone. However, there was an equally strong argument that she was now an even greater prize. Anyone could be tempted by a queen's ransom, or if they were truly evil: strike a terrible blow by murdering a king's fated mate, for without cubs, it would throw succession into chaos. She was very much afraid Guy Saville viewed her as the latter, especially if he had ambitions beyond the Eastern Lands.

Tyrants always wanted more.

Willie cleared his throat, then bowed. "Well, I know King Alaric wishes to depart very soon to allow the greatest amount of travel in daylight. Today you'll go to Worcester. After that to Gloucester, then a few days at the Forest of Dean for some excellent hunting and hospitality at St. Briavels Castle. I know there'll be many dignitaries for you to meet. Perhaps even some humans."

Evaine couldn't conceal a grimace. "Oh."

The marshal laughed. "Fear not, my queen, they would all have heard by now what happens to those who displease King Alaric. The Oxfords got what they deserved! I know it's not usually the Beaumont way, but we were all proud of our king for his small show of force. Sometimes it is necessary to remind others that just because a wolf prefers peace, he is by no means weak."

Except if the human is powerful, and so aggrieved that it starts a war.

Abruptly chilled, even wrapped up warmly in a hooded, ermine-lined black cloak, Evaine rubbed her gloved hands together. Although there had been no human retaliation, or further contact by an emissary or King Henry himself, she didn't believe for a moment that the matter was laid to rest. Not for an arrogant nobleman like Lord Oxford. "I suppose my main task is remembering I'm a duchess if around humans."

Willie's lip curled. "Bardy and I will never forgive the human king for such an insult. Why could Henry not just say 'I am battle-poor, leave your gold pile here'? No need to bring a worthless title into it. Poor King Alaric. Not like he could refuse."

Evaine nodded. Indeed he could not. But it was troubling that her mate had navigated *that* tricky situation yet not the Oxfords' comments about their mating ceremony. Did Alaric regret his actions? Was the lapse in judgment with the earl and countess the reason why he wished to keep some thoughts private from her?

In all honesty, he wouldn't be terribly aggrieved if she couldn't hear everything.

Unfortunately, the memory was burned in her brain alongside the perfection of their bonded mating. How could she tell Alaric she'd heard that thought with absolute clarity, not just the ones he wanted her to hear? Goddess, she hated pretending. Hated lying. But perhaps her mate simply required more time to know he could trust her. That she wasn't too delicate or too foolish to know everything. So for now, Alaric would be given the grace to be a right royal arse as Siân had so humorously described it. In future, she might have to take one of those solid gold plates and lovingly knock some sense into his stubborn Welsh skull.

"Will the king and I be on horseback?" asked Evaine. "Or travel in a covered wagon?"

"Your choice, really," said Willie. "There'll be fresh horses at each stop; in some places the roads might be impassable for a heavy cart. It depends on the weather, how much rain or snow, if the landowner has a care for the roads nearby. But it will be very cold and damp. And in some places...er...well, you're very precious, my queen. I heard those words from the king himself."

Warmth surrounded her heart and lifted her spirits. All would be well. A crowned queen certainly couldn't hide in a castle her entire life, nor would she want to. Not Evaine the Bold. "The king knows his lands far better than I do. I'll look to him for guidance."

About an hour later, as the sun began to rise, the procession departed Blackstone Castle, the gold-and-black flags of the Beaumont pack fluttering in the cool breeze. Siân would remain to oversee Blackstone along with Rowan, Oliver and Bardolf, while Evaine and Alaric had the services of Wesley, Blanche, Larkin the chamberlain and Willie to ensure the journey progressed smoothly. As they would be staying at castles and manor houses along the way, they didn't need to bring a great deal of food, but one cart near-groaned with barrels of wine, gold plate, goblets, eating knives and spoons, and napkins if needed. They also had their own sheets and pillows, something Evaine was very grateful for. She'd become shamefully particular after sleeping on such fine linen.

Another cart carried chests with her clothing: shifts and petticoats, gowns and shoes, gloves and wool stockings, and cloaks. A separate locked chest held a selection of jewels: necklaces and bracelets and rings, and her new diamond-studded circlet crown that she would wear to each gathering. Alaric had his own clothing cart, and other carts carried gifts to be distributed to his subjects. There was also an eye-watering collection of weapons such as extra swords, daggers, bows and arrows, pikes, maces, and shields. All the carts were covered in heavy canvas to keep the weather out.

Evaine and Alaric, Wesley, Blanche, Larkin, and Willie

had all chosen to ride horseback to Worcester, about a twenty-mile journey from Blackstone. However, there were also two well-appointed wooden wagons with a door and small windows covered by canvas that could be rolled up for fresh air. Inside there were cushioned bench seats, furs for warmth, flagons of mulled wine, and parcels of honey cakes and dried meats to ease hunger.

Goddess. No wonder Willie appeared a little fatigued— what he had organized in such a short time was quite frankly, a miracle.

"Are you ready, my queen?"

Alaric's voice, low and amused next to her ear, startled her out of her thoughts. How could just his voice make her heart beat faster? Especially when she was both hurt and irritated by his opinion on sharing thoughts through their bond link.

"I...ah...yes, of course," Evaine replied, a little flustered.

"You were studying the carts," he continued, his eyes glinting. "I promise Willie has thought of everything and then some. And we have ample gold to purchase any item we do not have."

"Good," she said crisply, grasping her horse's reins tighter. "Then let's not tarry about in the cold. Onward."

Alaric nodded then tilted his head back and howled, a raw, guttural sound that seemed to carry for miles. Now, everyone around would know, the King and Queen of the Western Lands were officially on progress.

Leto protect them.

―――

St. Briavels Castle, Gloucestershire

It wasn't Blackstone, but never had Alaric been so glad to see a castle.

While he'd enjoyed Worcester and Gloucester—both possessed cathedrals so majestic even wolves with no attachment to "God" or the "Holy Trinity" were compelled to stop and admire the craftsmanship—Gloucester had been especially difficult. Theda's family had long since fled abroad, but he would forever associate the place with her. In truth, he'd been genuinely shocked when Larkin asked if he wished to lay flowers upon her tomb. The thought was abhorrent, but Alaric at least had the excuse of dozens of meetings and audiences, and Larkin did beg forgiveness for the blunder.

Perhaps Alaric was just irritable without his queen.

The past few days had been nothing but duty and travel. His palm ached from shaking hands, his throat felt raw from speaking, and he'd spent countless hours in damp, shadowy rooms signing documents, judging disputes, receiving dignitaries, and hearing fresh reports from border guards on mercenary sightings or attacks. Evaine hadn't fared any easier; convening her first Western Council meeting, where she-wolves discussed battle training, trade, elder care, education, medical advances, upcoming state visits, and notable events since last time. By all accounts his mate had excelled, and he was very proud.

But now, after following the River Severn from Gloucester then cutting inland, they'd arrived at St. Briavels Castle and he could *show* her.

As their procession approached the huge double gatehouse fashioned of red sandstone and local limestone, Alaric's spirits lifted. The Forest of Dean was truly beautiful: fresh air, plentiful game, and no large hordes of humans.

Wesley rode up, fresh and jaunty as only a wolfling

could be. "My king, we have circled the area. It is completely secure. Shall I inform the queen?"

"Yes, do," said Alaric, glancing back at the covered wagon sheltering his mate. Rain had settled in just after they'd departed Gloucester and Blanche had bundled Evaine into the wagon to protect her fine clothing. No doubt she was clawing at the wood to get out; no wolf would ever choose slow, bone-jolting wagon over horse-back or run.

As the castle drawbridge was already lowered, the procession passed over the deep moat and entered the outer courtyard. Soon after, the Warden of the Forest of Dean and Constable of the Castle, Robert Poyntz, stepped out with his mate Margaret, and several of their cubs. All beamed and waved enthusiastically in greeting.

Alaric dismounted from his horse, grimacing at the cling of his wet, mud-splattered clothing, and his stiff muscles. Then he turned and helped an equally unhappy Evaine out of the wagon. A hot bath and time to really talk would cure these ills. After linking arms, they approached the Poyntz pack, who immediately dropped to one knee.

"My king," said Robert. "You honor us with this visit."

"Our pleasure to be here," said Alaric. "And it is my honor to present Queen Evaine."

Robert smiled. "My queen. You are thrice a miracle, to be found, restored to position, and now ruling us on the Western throne. Leto has blessed us all. Here is my beloved mate, Margaret."

After exchanging informal forehead presses and giving gifts to the excited cubs, Robert gestured for them to enter the gatehouse. "My king, we've prepared your usual rooms on the upper floor. Would you both prefer to rest and refresh before supper? Or stroll about the keep, perhaps?

We'll rise early tomorrow to hunt; I'm sure the weather will be much improved."

Alaric nodded, eager to be alone with Evaine. Their recent time apart only reminded him of the frantic week before the ceremonies, and he was frustrated beyond belief. "Rest and refreshment sounds ideal. Lead on, Rob...beg pardon, *Sir* Robert?"

The warden chuckled as they walked up the narrow spiral staircase. "Ugh yes, the human king awarded me a knighthood. Could be worse, though, Henry could have made me a *duke* at Bosworth Field! Unfortunately my wolf strength and skill set me apart; I wasn't even trying. But Henry promises peace, and Leto knows this realm needs it. Damned Yorks and Lancasters and their quarrels...ah, here we go. I hope it meets your approval, my queen."

Evaine entered the spacious, airy chamber and after inspecting the sturdy four-poster bed and the magnificent forest view, went straight to the fireplace. Closing her eyes, she sighed happily at the blazing warmth. "Lovely."

Alaric smiled at the sight. "Thank you, Robert. We'll see you both for supper."

The warden bowed. "My servants will bring up whatever you need from the wagons. Enjoy."

As soon as Robert departed, Alaric gathered Evaine in his arms and kissed her soundly. She melted against him, twining her arms about his neck.

Eventually she drew back, her eyes sparkling. "I needed that so much, I'll even accept the odor of wet fabric. You desperately require a bath, my king."

He removed his cloak, his cock already hardening. "Our hosts have kindly provided soap, sponge and hot water. Be thorough, my queen."

Evaine moaned softly. "I'm going to suck—"

At a sudden frantic knock, they both glared at the door.

"Yes?" barked Alaric.

"Forgive me, my king," came Robert's muffled voice. "I must speak with you urgently."

Evaine stepped back reluctantly. "I'm sure he wouldn't interrupt unless it was important."

Alaric sighed and nodded. After adjusting his hose, he marched over and pulled open the door.

Robert looked grim. "Henry is here! I suppose it's his right, he does own this castle...but we received no prior word and he has no procession. Just four mounted yeomen."

Alaric snorted. "While you are excellent company, Robert, I don't believe the human king is here to drink ale and relive past battle glories. I've been waiting for this. Let us meet in a private chamber."

"Of course, my king," said the warden, before hurrying away.

Sighing again, Alaric turned to his mate. "Henry is not trustworthy and you are too precious. I should meet him alone."

Evaine hesitated, her brow furrowing. Then it smoothed, and she nodded. "As you wish. I'll stay here by the fire. Will you take Wesley?"

"No. If Henry has come alone, I must do the same. But I'll return as soon as I can," he promised, kissing her hand before departing the room and marching down the stairs.

Gah. The only annoyance about St. Briavels: how long the passage into the keep proper was. Over forty feet! As a royal hunting lodge, the place actually had *three* deadly portcullis for safety, and Alaric always kept one uneasy eye on the wrought iron spikes as he passed underneath.

Bloody damned humans. Why had Henry come?

Soon, Robert ushered Alaric into a small antechamber off the Great Hall. Henry waited inside, his hands wrapped around a tankard of steaming mulled wine. Both Alaric and the warden inclined their heads in a pretense of deference, but when Robert made to leave, the human king pointed to a chair. "Stay, Sir Robert."

The warden exchanged a glance with Alaric, then sat. "As Your Grace desires."

More curious than ever, Alaric pulled out a chair at the opposite end of the table and sank onto it. "Good afternoon, Your Grace."

"Blackstone," said Henry, as he sipped his mulled wine. "God's blood, that is good. Infernal rain never stops around here."

Alaric and Robert exchanged another glance.

The warden coughed. "Is aught amiss, Your Grace? I received no word you were coming."

Henry actually smiled. "Perhaps I merely desired some time alone, away from the royal court and wedding preparations. At one of *my* hunting lodges."

Weary of the game, Alaric slapped the table. "You wished to speak to me. I'm sure Lord Oxford wasted no time with his report."

Henry sat back as though relaxed, but his brown gaze was watchful. "Ah yes. That. A story so far-fetched he surely dreamed it. Imagine, a battle-hardened earl claiming he and his wife were picked up by the throat and shaken about like feather pillows. That would take *uncanny* strength. Even for a Welshman! Why, it sounds like one of the ancient myths my uncle Jasper told me around the campfire when we were in exile. I always pressed him for more tales about werewolves. Now, what was the word in Welsh? Bla... blade..."

Oh, this human was cunning.

"Blaidd-ddyn?" asked Alaric politely, as though the topic bored him.

"That's it! Apparently, they walk among us. Large creatures, with the strength of ten men and the ability to turn into wolves at will. Ruled by kings, worship an ancient Greek goddess, but unlike other realms, born rather than bitten or cursed...I always wondered if it might be true. Surely in Wales, the land of dragons and lake maidens, anything is possible. What say you, Blackstone?"

His heart thumping, Alaric studied the human intently. "I certainly agree that anything is possible, Your Grace. Werewolves...a Lancaster wedding a York and bringing peace to the realm..."

The heavy silence stretched as two kings assessed, measured, and judged the other. Robert hadn't so much as blinked, but sweat glistened at his temples.

Abruptly, Henry set down his tankard and cleared his throat. "The Oxfords were presumptuous to impose. I shall caution them to refrain from wine, lest they have more fanciful dreams. The English throne has enough enemies; I desire no more. Especially not...well. I propose we be friendly neighbors who tend our own gardens and strive not to encroach. Is that agreeable?"

"Quite," said Alaric, nodding slowly. "In that spirit, my mate...er, my *duchess* and I will certainly send a generous purse to celebrate your wedding once you receive papal dispensation."

"Thank you," said Henry, as he stood and bowed deeply. "I know Elizabeth will join me in receiving it most gladly. Good morrow, Blackstone. Sir Robert."

And with that, the human King of England departed the room.

Robert exhaled heavily and slumped in his chair. "Goddess. You were so *calm*, my king! My claws were all the way out and I nearly shredded my hose. I did not want to disembowel Henry Tudor, but..."

Alaric smiled and rotated his rigid shoulders. "I think he understood that was a distinct possibility and I'm glad he chose to extend a hand of friendship. It's rather even...we might have the strength, but he has the numbers. Now, shall we drink?"

"Several barrels. At least."

————

Wrinkling her nose at the sour wine smell, Evaine shook her head as she stared at the sleeping, softly snoring form of her mate. Fully illuminated in the pale, early dawn light streaming through the large gatehouse window, Alaric was half-dressed, wearing one boot, and lay exactly where Wesley and two sturdy guards had placed him mere hours ago, on a fur-covered pallet beside the smoldering fire.

The previous evening, she had initially been alarmed when so much time passed and Alaric didn't return. Then Margaret arrived, apologetically explaining that after Henry had departed, her mate and King Alaric had immediately opened a barrel of wine, and were now on their second. Although both she-wolves were deeply curious to know what had transpired, they decided to leave their mates be. After enjoying a delicious supper of roasted pork and hearty vegetable broth, and playing some games with the cubs, each retired to bed. Not even Alaric's high-spirited squire was foolish enough to put his drunk king into bed with her; no doubt Robert would be waking in an equally uncomfortable place with a sore back, roiling gut, and crumpled clothing after his night's efforts.

For now, Evaine was torn between tossing dried fruit at Alaric's partially opened mouth, emptying an entire bucket of frigid spring water onto his head, or perhaps sounding a horn next to his ear. Unlike him, she was rested, refreshed, and ready to hunt. It was entirely too long since she'd been able to do so, and her whole body nearly twitched with the desire to bound along a flattened forest track, to leap over rocks and fallen logs and tiny streams in pursuit of deer or wild boar. Her fangs were tingling at the thought of sinking into warm flesh, her claws ready to rake and shred.

She was a she-wolf, after all. A lean, nimble killer.

"Good morning, my queen."

Evaine swallowed a giggle. Her mate peered up at her with bleary, bloodshot eyes, the glittering gold currently dull. His glorious ebony hair was a matted mess, and his chin and jaw covered in beard shadow. "Good morning, Alaric," she trilled, loud enough to wake everyone in the gatehouse.

He winced. "Such cruelty toward your king. I suppose I should ask forgiveness for drinking with Robert rather than returning to your bed?"

Evaine rolled her eyes. "That depends," she replied sweetly. "Do you ever wish to return to it?"

Alaric struggled to a sitting position, groaned and clutched at his head, then looked at her so morosely that this time she couldn't hold in her laughter. "Do I truly look as bad as I feel? We should not have opened a third barrel. Foolish mistake."

"Yes, yes, and yes," said Evaine merrily, her heart softening enough to cross the chamber and fetch some fresh water for him to sip. "Here."

After taking several gulps, Alaric splashed the rest on his face. "Much better. I don't suppose now you'd like to give me that special sponge bath?"

"I think not," she said with an imperious glare. "It is dawn and time to hunt. If, however, you impress me in the forest, then I may consider...rewards."

A slow smile curled his lips. "Challenge accepted."

With Wesley's assistance, Alaric bathed swiftly and downed some foul-smelling tonic, then he and Evaine both dressed in heavy robes to walk downstairs. In the ground floor antechamber, they hung their robes on iron hooks provided, before changing into wolf form. These days it barely hurt at all, and Evaine tossed her head and arched her back, tapping her claws on the stone floor as she stretched. Indeed, after all the wagon travel and endless meeting rooms, she was eager to feel moss and dirt under her paws and the wind ruffle her fur. To be the hunter rather than the hunted.

Outside, it was cold and damp, but the sky was clearing and there was no snow underfoot. Perfect.

Robert, Margaret, Blanche, and Willie were also in wolf form and waiting for them, while Wesley and the ten armed guards who would accompany the party remained in human form on horseback, their swords and shields gleaming.

Alaric flashed his fangs. "We'll go in pairs; a bag of gold to the best kill. With all glory to Artemis, our goddess of the hunt, I hereby declare...onward!"

As they needed no horn or call, the group exploded into action. Robert and Margaret went left, Blanche and Willie went right, and Evaine and Alaric charged straight down the middle. Already Evaine could scent game in the air, and she bounded forward, wanting to yip in delight at the prospect of bringing down a stag or wild boar.

"In which direction, my queen? I can see fresh antler marks on that great oak over there."

Evaine smiled as Alaric's voice reached her clearly through their link. *"Bah, only a six-pointer. I'll find real game for my bag of gold."*

"I'll give you gold. I brought along a certain toy you like," purred Alaric.

She almost faltered at the heady memory. Wicked wolf, trying to distract her from winning! *"You'll have to do better than that, my king."*

"Then lead on," he replied. *"Just look out for adders napping in the greenery or in hollow logs, they are common around here. While adders prefer to hiss in warning rather than attack, if you step on them or try to pick them up, they'll strike."*

Evaine shuddered. While royal wolves couldn't perish from snake venom, it would still hurt a great deal. *"I understand."*

For the next hour they loped along, sniffing the air and listening for prey. At this pace they could hunt all day, but she wanted to win the contest well before then.

Abruptly alert, Alaric lifted his head. *"A herd."*

Evaine inhaled deeply and her heart began pounding with excitement. Deer, at least five or six, including a full-grown stag, less than a mile away. *"Let's isolate him."*

The battle was surprisingly short; several loud snarls frightened away the rest of the herd. Although the stag stood its ground, bellowing and pawing at the earth with one hoof as it dipped its eight-point antlers, Evaine and Alaric continued to circle it, gradually drawing closer and closer. Then, when the stag attempted to flee through a small clearing, they charged after it, easily keeping pace.

"*Go, my queen,*" said Alaric. "*Now.*"

Evaine sprang, her powerful hind legs launching her onto the stag's rear, and she soon brought the beast down. Alaric ended its life, then he threw back his head and roared in triumph. Once Wesley and the guards appeared, Alaric gestured for his squire to cut two wooden poles to transport the stag back to the castle to be prepared for a feast.

Content beyond words at such a successful hunt, and the way they had so easily worked together, Evaine licked her muzzle and sighed. "*Magnificent.*"

"*You were magnificent,*" said Alaric, his gaze admiring. "*I've never enjoyed a hunt more. Perhaps we could do this again.*"

She twitched her tail, both annoyed and saddened at his hesitancy. "*We will do this regularly, Alaric. That is what bonded mates do. They spend a great deal of time together, in bed and out. They share their joys and sorrows, their burdens and victories. All of them. How can we continue to grow our bond if you conceal your thoughts from me?*"

Alaric bowed his head, his massive torso slumping a little. "*You heard.*"

"*Of course I heard,*" Evaine snapped at her very own right royal arse. "*But what really matters...your actions henceforth.*"

Her mate straightened and padded over, nuzzling his cheek against hers. "*Evaine the Bold. I will need the occasional reminder, until it lodges in my skull. Sharing everything is not easy for a wolf who has always worn a diplomat's mask. But I do feel. As you saw with the Oxfords,*" he finished ruefully.

"*And so, Alaric?*" she replied pertly.

"*Let me make it up to you.*"

Evaine licked him in return, a little approval grooming. "*With a bag of gold?*"

He growled, her favorite sound in the world. *"Among other things."*

Surrounded by their guards and with Wesley leading the way, they ambled back toward the castle, even stopping several times to rest under the rustling beech trees that flourished in the forest. At the keep wall, Robert and Margaret stood next to their six-point stag while Blanche and Willie had brought down a rather impressive wild boar, but all agreed that Evaine's eight-pointer won the gold.

Robert nudged his mate, then dropped his head in a wolf bow. "A magnificent morning's work. But please excuse us, castle duties await."

Alaric snorted softly. *"And by castle duties they mean rut."*

Somehow, Evaine didn't giggle. "Of course," she replied graciously. "Blanche, Willie, Wesley, I'm sure you have tasks of your own. The king and I will be in our rooms."

Outside the gatehouse, two servants waited with wooden buckets of warm water to rinse Evaine and Alaric clean. Then they entered the ground floor antechamber and changed back to human form. Alaric swiftly put his robe on, but when Evaine reached for hers, a small square of parchment dropped onto the floor.

"What's that?" he asked curiously.

Evaine frowned. "I don't know," she replied slowly, unfolding the square, then walking over to the small window for better light to read.

Queen Evaine,

Nothing is as it seems. The king will do to you what he did to Theda. If you wish to know more, wrap a note around a stone and drop it from your chamber window. I am prepared to meet any place, at any time.

A friend

Shock robbed her of breath. While every wolf in the Western Lands knew where they were, who could come so close to put a note in her robe? And make such an outrageous claim?

"Evaine?" said Alaric sharply. "What is it?"

She handed over the note. "Read it."

Shortly afterward, he sucked in a breath. "They dare imply I killed Theda?"

Evaine met her mate's furious gaze, her own grimly thoughtful. "Someone holds great malice toward you. Who would say such things yet claim to be a friend?"

CHAPTER
NINE

South Wales

If humans truly wanted to defeat wolves, no bloodshed was required. Why waste strength on battle when forced wagon travel would turn any wolf quite mad?

Alaric scowled as he lifted the canvas cover and peered out at the beautiful rainswept countryside. Usually he would be on horseback, galloping his way around South Wales from Newport to Cardiff to Swansea in a few days. Instead, because Willie and his guards held such grave fears for his and Evaine's safety after that strange note, they'd both been trapped in this torture device called a covered travel wagon for an entire damned week.

They'd both left Swansea very reluctantly; Evaine had been especially enamored of cockles gathered fresh from the bay and they'd devoured a small mountain, delighting in the change from venison, pork, and beef. But once again at dawn this morning, they had asked their bodies for forgiveness then climbed into the wagon for the next portion of the journey. This time: to the ancient town of Carmarthen. While it was only about thirty miles or so, Alaric desperately needed a distraction from the creaking and jolting and swaying. How did wagons manage to hit every rock and rut in the road with such precision?

Evaine scowled as she attempted for the thousandth time to find a more comfortable sitting position. "I really don't know why we must continue traveling in this monstrous wooden trap. Surely if there was a threat, they would have struck in the places with a much larger population to disappear into. I swear my arse will be black and blue from this bench seat."

"I know," he replied, irritable beyond belief. "Yes, a royal progress requires constant travel, but there is no need to make it worse with *wagons*."

"And it was just a note, promising information if I met with them. Not an actual threat."

Alaric refastened the canvas flap, then settled back on the seat which still felt harder than stone despite the cushions. Even thinking about that damned note made him angry. Perhaps it hadn't outright stated he'd had his first queen killed, but the implication was certainly there. Theda's death—he couldn't bring himself to call her his mate any longer—had occurred after a visit to Silas, her personal soothsayer. Silas had sworn under oath that Theda's death was accidental, but had fled Blackstone the next day. If anything was suspicious, surely it was that!

"I know we discussed it until we were hoarse," he said slowly, "but perhaps it would have been better to at least discover who the *friend* was. If they had any information about Silas. There are so many questions to be answered."

Evaine leaned forward and patted his knee. "No. As you

said, nothing was certain. We didn't know if they even were a friend, some brigand wanting coin, or a mercenary tricking me out into the open. In truth, I'm far more concerned that a guard or trusted servant was persuaded by a stranger to put that note into my robe."

"Unless it wasn't a stranger," said Alaric. Abruptly needing his mate closer, he took her hand and tugged her onto his lap so her knees were parted either side of his, and she could rest her head on his shoulder. As her delicious scent surrounded him, both soothing and sensual, his spirits soon lifted. "By the by, I might have an idea to pass the time."

His mate leaned back a little, her eyes glinting with mischief. "I'm sure you do, my king. But I can think of a better one: tell me something interesting about Carmarthen, and...I'll raise my gown."

Alaric straightened. His mate truly was the most brilliant she-wolf in the realm. "Some say it's the oldest town in Wales."

She wrinkled her nose, then wickedly rubbed her breasts against his chest. "I said something *interesting*."

His cock stirred. Goddess, even now the heady, musky fragrance of her cunt was drifting up to his nose. "Kings need inspiration. Show me your breasts."

With a sly grin, Evaine lowered and raised her gown's square bodice, teasing him with brief glimpses of her sweet pale pink nipples. Unable to resist, he clamped one hand around the back of her neck to hold her in place, then used his other hand to wrench down the velvet and fully reveal his treat. When he took one nipple in his mouth, flicking it with his tongue, even nipping it with his teeth, Evaine moaned and moved restlessly on his lap. "Suck me."

"Edmund Tudor, the human king's father, died of the

plague in Carmarthen," Alaric began, between rough, hard suckles. "He's buried there in a tomb within the Greyfriars church."

"Rather dark, but a start," she replied, her head falling back a little, one hand cupping her breast to offer him easier access while her other hand gripped his shoulder for balance. "I'm sure you can think of something better."

Sliding his hand down her back, Alaric lightly slapped Evaine's arse until she rose up on her knees, and he could move the fabric of her gown aside without tearing it. Then he delved underneath, greatly enjoying the discretion: even if someone could peer into the wagon, his actions were hidden. Only he and Evaine knew that he was trailing circles along her inner thigh, inching closer and closer to her hot, wet center.

"Hmmm," Alaric mused as he brushed his knuckles back and forth against her bush before parting the crisp hair and pushing his finger deeply inside her slick cunt, making her cry out. "Oh, do you need more fingers, sweetheart?"

"I want to spend. Hurry," Evaine said, attempting to grind down onto his finger.

Smiling inwardly, he withdrew it, to instead circle her pleasure bud. "But I just thought of something interesting, my queen."

"It better...oh, it better be...so, so good," she snarled, panting for breath.

"Allegedly, Merlin was born in a cave just outside of Carmarthen."

"I like that...oooohhhhhhh," Evaine gasped as he knit three fingers together and plunged them deep into her sheath.

"Now, sweetheart," Alaric murmured against her neck,

kissing the silken flesh as he twisted his fingers and nudged her bud with his thumb. "You must be quiet. No wild cries or the guards will come running."

To his great satisfaction, Evaine surrendered within moments to his tender ministrations, burying her face in his neck and screaming her release into his shoulder as her cunt spasmed around his fingers. How gloriously lusty she was! He truly adored how Evaine could be so fierce and bold, yet also submit so readily and completely to his touch.

When she moved on his lap, he grimaced as his cock strained against his hose, eager to be inside her. No. Not here. They were too close to Carmarthen to be knotted together when they arrived.

Evaine curled her hand around his cock. "What about you?"

His breath hissed between his teeth. "I'll be quite well."

"Doesn't feel like it," she replied saucily. "Now, the knotting aspect only happens when your cock is in my cunt, yes? For conception? What if...what if you spent in my arse? I liked the gold dildo in there. I wouldn't mind trying something much bigger, as long as you go slowly."

His blood surged at the delectable thought. Goddess, he might not survive. "You don't have to."

Evaine smacked his shoulder. "I know. I'm *offering*."

"I'll be so gentle," Alaric mumbled, even as he nearly tore the ties of his hose. "Go up on your knees again, Evie, I need to wet my cock in your honey."

Taking a deep breath in a futile attempt at regaining composure, Alaric gripped his swollen member and guided it between Evaine's legs. With the constant rattle and sway of the wagon it was almost impossible to be controlled, but he braced his feet against the base of the opposite bench seat for balance. Teasing them both, he swirled his cock in her copious juices, ensuring he coated as much of his length as possible.

"Do it," Evaine begged as she rubbed feverishly against him. "I want to feel you inside me."

By touch alone under her clothing, Alaric spread more wetness around her tight anus. Then he cautiously pressed a finger inside, easing it in and out until her inner walls seemed to welcome him rather than halt his advance. Goddess, he was so aroused he could scarcely see, and his mate's needy whimpers, her panting gasps as her hips churned, would be engraved in his mind forever.

"Hold on, sweetheart," he rasped. "I'll enter you now."

As he fitted the head of his cock to her anus and pressed in firmly, Evaine groaned, her back arching. Yet at the same time she pushed back on him, and soon the entire head was lodged snugly in her arse. Slowly, so slowly, Alaric carefully but relentlessly forced his cock a little deeper. The sensation was beyond words; she was so tight, so hot, it was all he could do not to spend at once and disgrace himself completely. But he needed to move. Every instinct insisted upon it, and he gently withdrew then advanced again.

"*Goddess*," said Evaine unsteadily as she rocked her hips. "It's like the biting ceremony. Pleasure and pain inter-twined. The stretch burns, but it feels so good, too. Keep doing that. Don't you dare stop."

"Oh, you like that, my queen?" Alaric growled as he thrust harder and harder, burying his cock as deep as it could go. "My cock in your arse?"

"Yes," she sobbed, her fingernails biting into his shoulders. "*Yes.*"

A heartbeat later, Evaine burrowed against his neck once again to muffle her scream of pleasure. The startling ecstasy of her fangs lightly scraping his flesh unleashed Alaric's own release, and his seed exploded inside her.

Utterly exhausted in the best way, Alaric rested his head against the wagon's carved wood wall and lifted one hand to stroke Evaine's back. "I just thought of another interesting Carmarthen fact for you," he murmured, between kisses. "It's where the King and Queen of the Western Lands enjoyed a most excellent wagon experience."

She giggled. "I like that one best of all."

———

"And how are you enjoying your stay in Carmarthen, my queen?"

Evaine smiled at the gathering of she-wolves, both younger and elders, as though she'd not already been asked the question ten times, and about one hundred times in each place they stopped on this progress. One important thing she'd learned: an audience really didn't care what she liked, as long as she praised it lavishly. "Carmarthen is a lovely town indeed," she replied. "Why, this manor house is simply delightful. So warm! And a charming view of the river."

In truth, the house *was* delightful, two levels fashioned of white stone with large timber-framed windows, and built on a rise so the views were sweeping. The bedchamber reserved for royal visits was on the upper floor, spacious yet cozy, and boasted a splendidly large and soft bed which was entirely welcome after all their wagon travel. Carmarthen was different to most of their stops, though, for the local castle here was actually a human stronghold and wolves in the area tended to stay well away from it. Instead, they gathered at various manor houses, the females descending on solars to drink wine, eat honey cakes, listen to music, and discuss any matters they didn't wish males or curious cubs to hear.

"And how does the king find our town this visit?" asked an elder eagerly.

Evaine almost blushed. She was still a little tender from their exertions in the wagon. "I know he has an even greater fondness for it."

There was a collective sigh, and similar to all previous stops, she was forced to conceal her reaction as the she-wolves began openly discussing Alaric's attributes: his smile, the sheen of his hair, the gold of his eyes, how tall and broad of shoulder he was, even the firmness of his arse. Wolves were frank about such matters and while Alaric tended to shrug it away, she might have to challenge someone to a duel...or at least bare some queenly fangs and claws. Those broad shoulders and firm arse belonged entirely to her!

"I'm going to bang some heads together," Blanche muttered beside her.

"Perhaps some music?" said Evaine, a little desperately as her claws dug into her palms. A certain blond female sitting in the corner and waxing lyrical about her king's lips would soon be losing a large clump of hair. "I do adore the harp...or the flute..."

A trifle grudgingly, the elder of the manor called for music. Soon, the glorious low tones of the harp filled the solar, and even more glorious, a chorus of voices in accompaniment. One thing Evaine had noticed throughout their travels: the Welsh loved to sing and were breathtakingly talented. While she didn't yet understand many Welsh words, there was a cadence to the ancient language, the way soft sounds flowed into one another and even harsh sounds were melodic, that made English seem just a bit awkward. It was the same when Alaric spoke on the most mundane matters, his words had a lilt that made them seem sensual. On several occasions she'd been so distracted by his accent that she'd completely forgotten the topic of conversation.

"Beg pardon, my queen."

Gritting her teeth at the interruption, Evaine turned to the hovering servant. "Yes?"

"Would you come and greet a group of peasants outside? They do not wish to intrude on manor land, but would like to make their bows and curtsies to the new queen."

Evaine frowned inwardly. It was an odd request; in planning for the progress, she and Alaric had specifically instructed that there be a large number of informal gatherings so all wolves were welcome. Naturally, the royal guards insisted any potential weapons be set down first, but certainly no one had been refused entry because they weren't landowners, wealthy or noble. Goddess, her own beloved mother had worked in a tavern! "Right now?"

"The family do not have much time, my queen, but they beg you to grace them with your presence," said the servant smoothly. Almost too smoothly.

The back of her neck prickled. Could this somehow be related to the note? Perhaps this was the opportunity to discover the identity of their "friend" and get answers once and for all.

"Very well," said Evaine, before turning to Blanche. "I'm going to greet some subjects outside, but will return shortly."

The elder wolf hesitated. "Would you like me to accompany you?"

Evaine shook her head. "Stay here and enjoy the music. I won't linger, I swear."

Soon, the servant guided Evaine outside to a well-tended enclosed garden. On the other side of the fence, a small group waited, cheering loudly as Evaine approached.

"Evaine is queen. Long may she reign!" called one male, and the two neatly-dressed cubs next to him waved madly.

Charmed, Evaine walked to the fence. Their awe was palpable as they expressed their best wishes, and she enquired after the male's mate and admired the cubs' wooden toys. Just as she was about to scold herself for being so foolish, a silver-haired male joined the group, wearing the dark robe of a soothsayer.

"My queen," he said with a low bow. "I am honored to be near you. Might I offer a blessing?"

Every instinct Evaine possessed bellowed *no*. But due to their connection to Leto, it would be frowned upon by all if she refused a soothsayer, so Evaine moved along the fence line until she faced him directly. "Good afternoon."

"Your hand?" he continued, his tone pleasant but his gaze piercing. Ugh.

"I have but a few moments," Evaine replied, reluctantly holding out her hand. Now that the friendly little pack had departed, the garden didn't seem nearly so lovely, just cold and isolated. And where were her two guards?

True alarm jangled through her body, but before she could turn and leave, the soothsayer grasped her hand. His palm was damp, his grip far too firm, then he leaned close. "My name is Silas. You are in grave danger, my queen. I hoped we might meet at St. Briavels, but alas, you chose to ignore my generous offer. I know all. I know the truth about Queen Theda's death, and that the same fate will befall you. The king is a killer."

What?

"Only Leto knows all. How dare you," Evaine snapped, both shocked and furious at his words. Yet she couldn't free her hand from the soothsayer's now-painful grip.

"I dare, because you must be told. Queen Theda did not fall down stairs—she was pushed. Murdered. A good female, cruelly treated by a cold male with a hot temper. You've seen the king's rage. Lord and Lady Oxford experienced it, did they not? He nearly strangled them both."

Even as she reeled at the accusations and his startlingly intimate knowledge of the humans' visit, Evaine managed to glare at Silas. "*A good female*? Theda was a scheming liar who tricked her way onto the throne. And you seem no better, fleeing Blackstone so swiftly after her death."

The elder's gaze shifted left and right before settling on her once more. "Those who carry words of divine wisdom are often called to walk a new path. But beware of the king, or *you* will end up on the floor with a face the color of wine."

Somehow, she laughed. "I have naught to fear from King Alaric. But you do. When he finds you..."

"Ah, I understand now," said Silas softly. "You're as mad as he is. I was wrong to appeal to a rational mind when you do not possess one. But it matters not. King Alaric...no, I'll not call him king. The *Duke of Blackstone* is weak and will soon be removed from power. I see battle. I see death. I see your sister Isabel, on her knees sobbing—"

"Stop," snarled Evaine, bracing her feet before twisting her wrist and tearing it from his grasp. "Leave these lands and never return. You are *banished*. If you are ever seen again, telling such evil lies, I will personally rip your heart out."

"It is too late," the soothsayer replied, bowing once

more, his eyes aglow. "A mighty boulder is rolling down a hill and cannot be halted. Soon there will come a reckoning between yourself and King Guy."

"The usurper? No. There is only one true King of the Eastern Lands," said Evaine, her claws extending. "Lucan de Wynter. My brother will return."

"Your brother is dead. King Guy has waited a long time to see you fall, and fall you shall. With the Book of Lore at his command, the throne of the Western Lands will be his as well. Enjoy the rest of your progress...*Duchess*."

And with that, Silas strolled away as though he hadn't a care in the world.

Her limbs trembling, Evaine collapsed onto a nearby garden bench, sucking in gulps of air as rage and fear twisted inside her belly. A part of her had always known that one day she would meet Guy Saville again. But was she ready to face that vile murderer in battle? And how would Alaric react, knowing the missing soothsayer who may have witnessed or even caused Theda's death had returned?

"Goddess," she whispered, wrapping her arms around herself and rocking on the bench. Right now it felt like she might never be warm again.

"My queen! Are you well?"

She glanced up to see the two missing guards sprint around the side of the manor house and hurry to where she sat. "Where were you?" Evaine cried. "Did you see that soothsayer? Did you stop him?"

One of the guards dropped to his knee, his expression confused. "Forgive us. We didn't see a soothsayer, but a servant claimed there was a male at the gate with a dagger, threatening harm. We thought you were safely upstairs listening to music with Mistress Blanche, so went to investigate. When we returned, that servant was nowhere to be found."

Evaine took several deep breaths, attempting to calm her jangled nerves. "Take me to where the king is holding his meeting. I must speak with him at once."

———

This meeting had dragged entirely too long, and he was entirely too far away from Evaine. Everything was colder and duller without his mate, including activities he'd previously tolerated or even enjoyed.

Alaric drummed his fingers impatiently on the heavy oak table in front of him and glared at the dozen male noble wolves who were currently arguing over a particularly foolish potential amendment to the Western Charter: whether soothsayer robes should continue to be black, or change to brown. How was this even an issue, let alone a topic worthy of debate? Listening to passionate declarations about fabric color was a truly torturous process—he was quite certain Evaine wasn't suffering so much with the she-wolves.

"Black!" he barked eventually. "The robes will remain black by royal decree. Now, are there any other matters of business, or can we adjourn?"

For a short while there was blessed silence, and Alaric almost stood and departed the damp and rather cool stone hall they were meeting in. It would probably be warmer to meet outside; this hall had just two fireplaces which wasn't nearly enough for the size of the room, and most of the nobles kept moving restlessly and pulling their cloaks tighter.

Unfortunately, one of the wolves to Alaric's left—a

landowner near Witney, very close to the border with both the Eastern and Southern Lands—cleared his throat. "My king, if I might have the floor?"

Alaric sighed at the wolf's tentative voice. Several present had used a similar tone today and while it was entirely his own fault, it still stung how fast his long-standing reputation for cool, calm diplomacy had been ruined by his actions toward the Oxfords. "Yes. Speak."

The wolf actually gulped as he rose to his feet. "My king. Fellow brethren. I know this remains a very sore wound in our history, however before I came here, I received yet another petition from an Eastern Lands emis-sary. They are requesting the resumption of trade and diplomatic ties with the Western Lands..."

A loud chorus of "NO" erupted until Alaric held up a hand. "Let him finish."

His face glistening with sweat, the landowner cleared his throat. "It has been ten years. While it brought us all great joy to learn Princess Evaine had survived her long ordeal, and to receive her as King Alaric's fated mate and our anointed queen...er...we have heard nothing of Prince Lucan. Not even a whisper. Is it time to accept Lord Guy Saville's claim by force and victory? The humans accepted Henry as their king after he killed Richard at Bosworth Field, and that was mere months ago."

Pure fury surged through Alaric, and he clenched his fists lest he hurl the oak table into the neighboring county. After what his precious Evaine had suffered, what her two missing sisters and brother continued to suffer...the murders of Hugo and Magdalena, and the constant threat of mercenaries hunting in Guy Saville's name for a bounty he would pay...there would be ice castles in the Persian desert before Alaric Dafydd Beaumont would break bread with *anyone* from that court.

"No," Alaric said slowly and clearly, so there was no chance of misunderstanding. "As long as I'm alive, the only claim to the Eastern throne my court and all my councils will recognize is that of King Lucan de Wynter. There is no comparison between Guy Saville and Henry Tudor. The usurper repaid generous favor with treachery and murder. The human king at least has a few drops of royal blood, but far more importantly, will wed a princess of the blood to secure his throne. Saville has neither."

"My king—"

"If King Lucan has in fact risen to the stars without an heir, then I would recognize Princess Isabel as Queen Regnant and her future line. After that, Princess Cecily and her future line. All before Guy Saville. In truth...I would recognize a half-eaten boar's tongue before Guy bloody Saville."

Complete silence filled the hall, and to his great dismay, Alaric realized his voice had been getting louder and louder, his last few words actually echoing around the room. Goddess. He may as well cease all diplomatic tasks immediately—he no longer possessed the skill or patience.

His longtime scribe, Peregrine, a plump, bald elder wolf with a grizzled gray beard and the most exquisite penmanship imaginable, looked up from his ink and parchment. "I believe King Alaric has made his thoughts on this matter very clear. On several occasions. If anyone requires assistance with their memory, say aye, and I'll engrave it on your forehead."

Alaric almost laughed. Indeed, there was a smattering of chuckles around the hall and it offered the chance to compose himself. While his opinion on Guy Saville would never change, and, he was quite certain, Evaine would concur, there was no need to roar at the messenger. That landowner clearly didn't want to bring the petition any more than Alaric wished to receive it.

"Forgive the thunderstorm," said Alaric ruefully, inclining his head in apology. "I am too long apart from my mate and quite out of sorts—"

"Alaric. Alaric, can you hear me?"

Evaine's voice burst so clearly into his mind that he actually looked around the room for her. Naturally, she wasn't there. *"Evie?"*

"Oh! You heard! I wasn't sure if our bond link would work this far apart."

"I don't know either," he admitted. *"Maybe there is a distance limit, or perhaps we can each be in any place. Where are you?"*

"On horseback, with my guards. We are about a half-mile away from you."

"Is something wrong?"

She paused briefly. *"I must speak with you. Urgently. Face to face."*

Alaric stood so fast that his chair actually wobbled, before righting itself with an audible slap onto the floor. "I must take my leave. The queen is on her way here and requests an audience at once."

All the dignitaries within the room stilled, their brows creasing in concern and surprise, and questions began firing at him like a flurry of arrows.

"Is our queen well?"

"Did something happen at the manor house?"

"Mercenaries? Surely they wouldn't dare."

Alaric clenched his jaw. "I believe Queen Evaine is

unharmed. But something has happened. As soon as I know, I will pass on any necessary information."

With that he turned on his boot heel and strode from the meeting, his speed increasing as he reached the hallway until he was leaping down the stairs and running for the front door, utterly uncaring if he knocked something over. He had one need: to see his mate, to know for certain that she was well. Evaine the Bold wouldn't ride to him without cause. If anyone had upset or hurt her, he would personally disembowel them.

It seemed to take forever, but at last three riders appeared over the rise, galloping toward the estate. Alaric waited as patiently as possible even as perspiration gathered at his neck. When they pulled up, he marched straight to Evaine and lifted her from her horse. Then he curled his arm around her waist and guided her into an empty antechamber inside the manor house.

"Tell me everything, sweetheart," he said simply.

Instead of answering, she wrapped her arms around his waist, burrowing against his chest. Instinctively, Alaric's arms closed around her, holding Evaine tightly until she stopped shaking. Then his mate leaned back a little, met his gaze, and said one word: "Silas."

Alaric froze. "Theda's soothsayer?"

"Yes," said Evaine, resting her cheek against his chest, her fingers restlessly tangling in his doublet fabric. "I was greeting a peasant family when he arrived...Silas lured me over by offering a blessing, then took my hand and wouldn't let go. He said the most terrible, wicked things. I... I banished him, said that if he ever returned, I would personally rip his heart out."

Alaric nodded at the fierce promise in his queen's voice. Indeed, his courageous, passionate Evaine would never shy from a battle. But he didn't like that she had skimmed over details like a rock bouncing across a stream. It was true: a strong bond meant sharing everything. "Good. Now tell me, what were the terrible, wicked things?"

Just briefly, her fingernails dug into his doublet. "They were about you. And Theda. Silas said you pushed her down the stairs and that I was next."

Alaric braced for another ragestorm to overcome him. Instead, a strange, eerie calm descended. "I will have his head for that," he said slowly. "Was there anything else?"

She nodded miserably. "Silas claimed there would soon be a reckoning between me and Guy Saville. A battle. And death. That we would be removed from power—with the help of the Book of Lore, Guy would take the throne instead."

Filthy. Wretched. Bastard.

Abruptly, Evaine laughed, the sound very watery. "Yes. Yes, he is."

Moving his hands to cup her face, Alaric blotted her tears with his thumbs, then leaned down and kissed her forehead. "You are more precious to me than all the gold in the Western Lands. Than Blackstone Castle. Anything or anyone. There is no way on Leto's earth that I will allow any harm to befall you. Do you understand, Evie? You are my queen. My fated mate. *Mine.*"

Evaine turned her head, her lips brushing his palm. "I understand, my king."

After taking her in his arms once again, they stood silently in the antechamber, just holding each other. But all the time, Alaric's mind raced. The latest overture from the Eastern Lands emissary for peace and trade resumption made a certain malevolent sense now. They held out their hand to shake, while hiding a dagger in their sleeve.

Well. If Guy Saville wanted a war, he would get one. And if he or his little soothsayer Silas thought to raid and conquer the Western Lands, they would soon learn in the most agonizing, bloody way what a mistake that would be.

The only question remaining: *when.*

TEN

Wolf's Gate, Chester, Northwest England

From this heavily fortified tower within the City Walls constructed centuries prior by the Romans, the view was nothing short of spectacular. Yet rather than a queen, Evaine now felt like a prisoner. The royal progress to meet her new subjects had become the stuff of bad dreams.

Alaric had summoned another fifty warriors to accompany them around the remaining stops in Wales; in the past two weeks they had continued on from Carmarthen to Cardigan, then more inland to Machynlleth and up to Bangor. Yet even when they changed lodgings or route, notes continued to arrive wherever they were, bleak and threatening, like they were being stalked. Either that or they had a traitor within the ranks, but Alaric refused to believe a member of his household would do so. Right now, she fully trusted no one other than her mate, Blanche, and perhaps young Wesley.

Worse, when Evaine woke earlier, she'd felt wretched with a nagging headache, aching limbs, and a mild fever that flared uncomfortably if she was even in the vicinity of a fireplace. In early February, Chester was much colder than the Welsh coast, but even in chilling winds she yearned to stand outside half-naked. If anyone complained, she would snatch up their hand and bite off a finger. Perhaps the entire arm if they were particularly vexing—and that included her mate.

Then again, it was far more than minor illness or the temperature outside keeping her and Alaric awake each night. Since crossing back into England, they barely slept or ate. Several banquets and meetings had been canceled, and even more warriors summoned from the surrounding towns and villages. The dark clouds of impending battle were gathering, and every Western wolf knew it.

"My queen..."

Evaine turned to see Wesley standing in the tower room doorway, his usual high spirits and mischief severely dampened in recent times. Even Alaric had admitted to wanting a prank or jest from his squire, just for the reminder that amusement was still possible. They all desperately needed it. "Come in," she said softly, gesturing to a wooden chair and pouring a goblet of mulled wine. "This will warm your innards."

The squire downed her offering in one hefty swallow, coughed a few times, then made a face. "I don't understand how people enjoy mulled wine. It tastes like someone mixed a few herbs with used bathwater."

At the hint of the old Wesley, she grinned. "Perhaps that is the secret ingredient. Now, tell me how the others fare. Truthfully."

"Hmmm," said the squire, tapping his chin. "Willie has

aged about a century in the past few weeks—Bardolf will be shocked when they reunite. Then again, perhaps he has a secret appreciation for newly silver fur and shadowed, bloodshot eyes."

Evaine barely concealed a wince. The marshal had perhaps suffered worst of all as he continually amended travel plans and organized more fortified lodgings, not to mention food and supplies for a significantly larger group. "Poor Willie. He is working very hard."

"Perhaps I shouldn't say this, but I know he and King Alaric have had words several times about ceasing the progress and returning to Blackstone Castle. My king says he cannot neglect a third of his realm for the sake of a few notes, and he's right, but..."

Evaine nodded. They were in an exceedingly difficult position. After Chester, the planned route included Liverpool, Preston, Lancaster, a special banquet at the most northern town, Carlisle, before traveling back down to Kendal, Bradford, Manchester, Stoke-on-Trent, Birmingham, then home. Another ten days at least. And while she absolutely understood the need for the king to be seen, for her to be accepted as queen, for meetings to be held and issues resolved, living like this brought back harrowing memories of her earlier years.

Perhaps it was time to stand firm and fight. To gather as many warriors as possible, on ground they knew, and lure their enemies to them instead of always reacting.

"How is Blanche?" she said instead. "And Larkin?"

Wesley sighed rather theatrically. "Unlike everyone else, Mother is eager and ready to lead an army. Alongside her duties with you, she ensures everyone has food and blankets, mends clothing, darns hose, sharpens swords and daggers, and portions out the ale. She scolds and praises and stands no nonsense; I'm convinced at least half the warriors are in love with her, which quite roils my gut."

Now Evaine did laugh. "That sounds like she has taken over Larkin's travel responsibilities. What is our chamberlain doing, then? Shoeing horses? A little carpentry?"

The squire hesitated. "In truth, my queen, I don't really know. We hardly see him. Larkin says he's on the king's business, and often rides out by himself. He's done that throughout the progress. And he writes mountains of letters. Once I asked who he was writing to so often, and he said wolflings were too foolish to know. But I'm not just any wolfling. I am the king's squire!"

Evaine's neck prickled and she rubbed it absently. Now that Wesley mentioned it, their chamberlain *was* often absent. Even on the king's business, it wasn't fair that Blanche was doing so much. If more messengers were needed, that could certainly be arranged. There was no reason for a castle chamberlain to be doing such menial tasks personally. Unless...

She shook her head to clear the thought. No. Any evidence was coincidental or hearsay at best. No wolf could be convicted on that. "And you are an excellent squire, Wesley. A credit to your sire and mother. Tell me, where is the king? He did mention something about sword practice this morning."

Wesley sprang to his feet. "Follow me, my queen! I'll take you straight to him. There is a room with no furniture that he has been using. Warriors take turns being his opponent, but, oh, King Alaric bests them all. He moves as one with a sword. I mean, he was *already* good, but whenever he sees King Darius, he gets more lessons and now he is brilliant."

Evaine suppressed a smile. The way Wesley worshiped

Alaric was rather endearing, and she absolutely understood the sentiment. Except during her mate's right royal arse moments, of course. "Let us go, then."

While Wesley bounded down the tower's spiral staircase, she was forced to move at an irritatingly sedate pace. Perhaps that should be a training method, warriors sword fighting while a gown train tangled about their legs, pointed shoes pinched their toes, and coiled braids slapped against their ears.

"It's just down here, past the portrait gallery," called the squire over his shoulder as he loped along a narrow hallway.

Hurrying after him as best she could, Evaine glanced up, her gaze settling on a portrait of Hugh d'Avranches, the first Norman Earl of Chester. Apparently, the humans called him Hugh the Wolf due to his ferocious fighting style, but wolves knew what he really was. If faced with their situation, Hugh would certainly charge on until the bitter end.

Ahead, Wesley abruptly halted beside a door, then bowed. "In here, my queen. Be careful, though, I can hear steel clashing."

Not wanting to interrupt and cause an accidental injury, Evaine tentatively pushed open the door. There was only one window, but with several candelabra lit, the room was brighter than a summer's day. The stench of tallow candles made her grimace but no one inside seemed to notice; two exhausted-looking warriors, one male and one female, sat slumped by the east wall, dripping with sweat and spotted with blood. In the center of the room, Alaric fought another male. Wesley spoke true: her mate was indeed brilliant.

It was astonishing how graceful such a large male could

be. Every step Alaric took seemed purposeful, he neither stood still nor bounced on his feet. But most impressive was the way he made the sword move with such deadly force: cutting and slashing yet easily deflecting his opponent's blade. Just when it appeared a blow might land, Alaric twisted away or sidestepped then immediately counter-attacked. When at last he dislodged the other male's sword and it fell to the stone floor with a loud clatter, Evaine couldn't help but applaud.

Alaric clapped the warrior on the shoulder. "Excellent work. You nearly had me there. But I must greet my queen. To the victor the spoils, madam?"

All the wolves grinned, clearly expecting a passionate kiss. Instead, Evaine scowled and wrinkled her nose. "Perhaps later, my king. After you've bathed."

His brow furrowing, Alaric dismissed the warriors with a wave of his hand then closed the door, giving them privacy. "You've never been upset by a little sweat before. What troubles you?"

"The same that troubles you," she grumbled. "An impending war. Deciding whether to continue the progress or return to Blackstone Castle."

"I heartily recommend sword fighting as a brief respite from thinking about either," he sighed, sheathing his longsword.

Evaine bit her lip as her temper flared again. No. Scolding him because she didn't feel well was unfair. And she had information her mate needed to know. Information possibly new to him. "Wesley came to visit. I think Blanche is scraping his last nerve."

Alaric chuckled. "I do feel for him. Adventures are not quite so amusing when your mother is there to clip your ear or cut your meat. Wolfling is such an awkward stage. They yearn for all the freedoms of full-grown wolves, yet still want to romp and provoke like cubs."

"Wesley said mulled wine tasted like someone added herbs to used bathwater," Evaine replied, smiling at the memory. Then she took a deep breath. "But he also said something else that gave me pause. About Larkin."

Her mate went still. "Go on."

"It started as Wesley muttering about his mother. But as he listed all the tasks she was doing, it sounded very much like those of a chamberlain. So I asked what Larkin was doing. And it seems he keeps going missing...on the king's business. Writing lots of letters and delivering them. Of course, this could be completely right and proper, and we're just seeing rats with any rustle."

Alaric didn't smile. "I haven't instructed him to write anything, Peregrine, my scribe, does that. And I have sufficient messengers. Larkin certainly isn't laboring on my behalf."

Evaine exhaled slowly. "Then whose?"

———

Was Larkin a traitor?

The question pounded Alaric's mind like a mallet. History bellowed *no;* Larkin had been born and cheerfully raised at Blackstone Castle. And apart from a few strange comments, such as placing flowers on Theda's tomb in Gloucester, Alaric had no real reason to distrust the chamberlain. Yet his actions were suspicious. Evaine had been entirely correct to bring such concerns to him.

"Damn it," he cursed. "I don't want to think badly of anyone in my household. But the way those bloody notes kept finding us, no matter where we were..."

Evaine nodded. "It has to be someone close enough to us that they can come and go freely. Who reports only to you or me. No one would question a chamberlain, and we've both been far too busy to notice what one wolf does."

"Then let him explain. Settle this once and for all," Alaric growled as he opened the door and peered out into the hallway. "Wesley, would you fetch Larkin? Tell him I wish to discuss an important matter. Er...a possible return to Blackstone."

Wesley bowed, his expression grave. "Yes, my king. At once."

It seemed like they waited years for his squire's return. Alaric's gut churned at the implications of such betrayal; all he and Evaine could do was exchange increasingly impatient and troubled glances as time passed. Finally, Wesley came hurtling around the corner, his boots skidding and cheeks flushed pink. But one glance at his squire's expression and Alaric's heart sank. "What news?"

"Larkin has departed with a cart, my king," said Wesley breathlessly. "About a half hour ago. He told a guard that you wished for fresh game, and he was going to collect it from *Huntington*."

"Is that a market of some sort?" asked Evaine, her brow furrowing.

"No, it's a small village about three miles from here, surrounded by woodland and meadows," said Alaric, increasingly alarmed. *Three miles!* Who was Larkin meeting? Only a supremely confident enemy would dare to venture so close!

Evaine took his hand and squeezed it, her expression grim. "If there is to be a battle, I suppose it is a blessing that this place is fairly isolated and not overrun with humans. But if mercenaries have been creeping in..."

"Then I must cull the herd," he replied harshly. "Wesley, come with me. Evie, I need you to command the tower. Inform Willie and Blanche and all the wolves here that if Larkin is found he must be immediately captured and imprisoned. If I gather further indisputable evidence, I shall amend the order to execute on sight."

She glared at him. "I should accompany you. I can hunt."

"I know. Bravely and fiercely," Alaric replied, cupping her cheek. "Once we have information on the nature and number of the enemy, you may rip as many hearts out as you wish. But for now, I need a commander here I can trust absolutely."

Evaine huffed out a sigh. "Very well. But do not tarry. And do not dare start a war without me."

"I swear, my queen," he promised, lifting her hand and kissing it. Then Alaric turned to Wesley. "Change into plain clothing and fetch your bow and arrow. We're going hunting."

After donning a warm cloak, Alaric marched to the rooms housing his guards. He selected four, ordering all to discard their black-and-gold livery and dress as peasants, and to pack a variety of weapons into saddlebags. At first glance, they should appear as nothing more than six friends or clerics out for a brisk ride, but they needed to be prepared for anything.

Soon, Alaric led a brisk canter to Huntington. Good fortune smiled upon them, for an hour later as they approached the woodland area, Wesley pointed out a cart traveling toward a simple stone cottage. Larkin! So bold and confident in his deceit, he'd not even bothered to cover his plaited red hair.

Concealing themselves in a thick clump of trees, the

group watched Larkin's cart pull up next to the cottage. He leaped down, then, after glancing left and right, sauntered toward the entrance. Two figures stepped out to greet him.

"Goddess," whispered Wesley. "It's Silas!"

Alaric cursed under his breath. Despite what he'd said to Evaine, even riding here, he'd hoped Larkin's behavior was innocent; just unlucky coincidences and a chamberlain trying to purchase better-quality meat. Or at worst, a lust-addled bachelor foolishly abandoning his duties to rut with a pretty female. But no. Larkin was a bloody traitor. He was the reason that walking sack of shit Silas had been able to send a note, then approach and threaten, the Queen of the Western Lands. Larkin was the reason their enemy always knew where they were.

The two males were even exchanging notes right now!

"Aye, would you look at that," said one of Alaric's guards with a low whistle. "So brazen."

"What orders, my king?" asked Wesley, moving restlessly in his saddle. "Attack and kill them all?"

"Not yet," said Alaric. "First, let's send them a gift of flaming arrows. If the cart and cottage are ablaze, we'll soon know how many there are. Wesley, I want you to shoot. You can crouch behind that small rise there."

His squire appeared briefly startled, then a huge grin lit up his face. After sliding from his horse, Wesley pulled his bow from its narrow wooden tube. He flexed his fingers and tested the string several times before turning back to Alaric, a look of grave concentration on his youthful face. "I'm ready, my king."

The second guard began preparing the arrows, first wrapping a short length of linen just beneath the head, then expertly dipping it in pitch. The third guard struck a flint against a rock until it created sparks, and once they had a flame, carefully lit an arrow before passing it to Wesley.

"Off you go, boyo," said Alaric. "Show us your arm. I know you've been practicing."

His squire's first attempt was short, landing harmlessly in mud, and Wesley's shoulders slumped. But he swiftly tried again, the second arrow flying straight into the cart and setting a pile of straw alight. The third scorched across the cottage roof, and the fourth, a truly admirable shot, sailed directly in the large open window. There was a yelp from inside the cottage, and two more males dashed out. Ah. Five in total.

"Wesley, fire at will," growled Alaric as he unsheathed his sword. "We'll ride around and meet those who flee with blades. Take Silas and Larkin alive, if possible—the rest are worthless. For the West!"

"For the West!" the guards and Wesley cheered.

Anticipation coursing through his veins, Alaric urged his horse forward. He crouched low as he kicked hard, the mighty steed galloping through the trees as though equally eager to spill blood. Already three of the enemy were attempting to escape on foot, while Larkin and Silas both had horses.

"You take the runners," called Alaric. "I'll go after Larkin and Silas."

Two guards nodded and expertly veered right to follow the three on foot. Alaric galloped on, and was soon nearly side by side with Larkin. The chamberlain might be competent inside a castle, but had never enjoyed riding. "Halt!"

Larkin turned his head and went ashen. "My king..."

"Traitor," Alaric snarled, leaning left to slash at the other wolf with his sword.

The chamberlain screeched in pain as blood oozed from

his side, but somehow managed to keep his seat. Then he reached down and pulled a length of heavy fabric from his saddlebag, before tossing it not at Alaric...but over the head of Alaric's mount. Immediately blinded, the horse reared in panic, and it took every bit of Alaric's strength and skill to hang on as his mount bucked and tossed its head. Eventually he was able to dislodge the fabric—to add insult to injury, a Beaumont flag—and calm his horse, but when he looked around, the two males he'd been pursuing were gone.

Alaric roared in frustration. So damned close but they'd slipped through his fingers. The one thought that cheered him: perhaps Larkin would succumb to his wound. Without the Book of Lore's protection, only wolves with royal blood had immunity to everything except beheading with a blade of pure silver.

But in truth, he'd failed. Two traitors might well return to sanctuary in the Eastern Lands, or rejoin their pack of mercenaries, wherever they were. Damn them both.

Very reluctantly, Alaric turned his horse and galloped back to the burning cottage.

Wesley rode up to meet him. "My king, are you well? I thought for certain you would be thrown!"

"I'm quite well," he replied, thoroughly irritated. "I just pray to Leto that Larkin's side wound grows putrid. How did the others fare?"

"Three enemy hearts to burn," said his squire. "We'll get Larkin and Silas next time, I swear it. I should have accompanied you and fired arrows directly into their arses."

"You've a great talent with the bow," said Alaric gruffly. "That arrow in the window...I could not have done better."

Wesley flushed bright red. "I much prefer bow to sword. I would piss my hose if I faced you in battle."

"Fortunately we're on the same side," he replied, cuffing his squire on the shoulder. "Now, that weak sun is not yet high in the sky, so let's return to the tower and I'll dispatch new orders."

Soon they were six again, riding in tight formation. No one had charged to assist their enemy, but any manner of creature could be lurking, just waiting for a chance to ambush them.

"Will you tell Mother?" asked Wesley unexpectedly.

Alaric raised a brow. "Do you want me to?" he countered.

"I think if there was a way you could make it clear I was far, far away from danger yet very, very brave and skilled?" asked the squire hopefully.

He laughed. "I'll think of something. As long as you never tell the queen I was defeated by a *flag*. She is already vexed with me today."

"All I remember is your excellent riding, my king. At least Queen Evaine is safe."

"Yes," said Alaric. "And no doubt eager to hear all the details. I'll regale her as soon as we return."

———

In the past few hours, Evaine and Blanche had nearly worn a path in the tower floor with their incessant pacing.

Evaine stared out the window overlooking the court-yard, her arms folded lest she hurl something breakable. "They should be back by now."

Pausing in her scrubbing of the table—probably the cleanest it had been in several centuries—Blanche attempted a smile. "At least an hour there and an hour back, my queen. Slower if the guards grew weary of my Wesley's chatter and tied him to a tree."

"Do you think they found Larkin? Would they fight him?" The questions burst from Evaine like a flurry of Wesley's arrows.

"Perhaps, if Larkin did go to Huntington. It's barely a village, more a scattering of cottages, and apart from the woodlands, there is nowhere else to hide. But the king would easily defeat him; Larkin is an indoor wolf, enamored of creature comforts. He won't even lift a paw to find his fated mate, says she is dead."

Evaine frowned. "Dead? But that is terrible!"

"Oh no, my queen, do not pity him. Larkin's great love story was entirely in his head. Lady Theda used him to get close to King Alaric, then afterward to serve her interests."

"Wait," said Evaine, her gaze narrowing. "*The* Theda?"

Blanche sighed. "To hear Larkin tell the tale, he was a chivalrous knight defeated by a taller, richer dragon at Gloucester. He won't hear a word against Lady Theda, especially not the truth: she was a scheming viper wanting only a queen's crown. Her death is all he speaks of, and despite his lofty position as king's chamberlain, no female will entertain his nonsense now. Well, that, and...er..."

"And what?"

The elder wolf flushed. "Beg pardon, but how poor a lover he is, my queen. Females call him Larkin Cwningen— that's 'rabbit' in Welsh—because he humps away and finishes in two tail twitches."

Evaine bit her lip, but a giggle burst forth, and soon both of them near-cried with uncontrollable laughter. "Oh my," she wheezed, trying to regain composure. "How unfortunate."

"It is," said Blanche, dabbing her eyes. "Both for those

robbed of pleasure and everyone else in the castle, for Larkin mopes about like a lovelorn swain. But he knows nothing of real love. It's not worshiping from afar, but standing together and accepting all the sunshine and storms that are sent. Seeing the beauty in moments: in a smile, in a service, in being truly seen and heard. Oliver makes me *howl* in bed. But best of all, he tolerates my foibles just as I tolerate his. We've navigated this journey together, indeed, for forty years I've been loved as a she-wolf should be. Fiercely. Passionately. Loyally. And along-side our cubs, that is the greatest blessing."

Evaine smiled wistfully. Alaric certainly ensured inde-scribable pleasure. He treated her as his equal, wasn't threatened by her talents, and called her precious. But did he love her? With fated mates, the knowledge that you *were* supposed to be joined was enough for many wolves. However, Mother and Father had told each other 'I love you' every day, and she'd always wanted the same. Bah. Perhaps she was just being ungrateful. The Western Lands needed a strong, sure queen, not a delicate daisy. "Oliver is fortunate, having such a wise and capable mate. Speaking of mates, should we send out a search party for the king? Ride out ourselves?"

Just as Blanche was about to reply, a male guard rapped on the door. "My queen—"

"King Alaric and Wesley are back? Oh, thank Leto for that. What news? Did they capture Larkin? Is he dead? What happened?"

The guard grimaced. "They've not yet returned, my queen. But a sealed note arrived. The messenger said it must be placed directly into your hand, no other."

Her heart pounding, Evaine reached for the neatly folded square of parchment that was secured with red wax.

Unlike most important missives, there was no crested ring or stamp in the wax to identify the sender.

She swallowed hard. "Is the messenger waiting for a reply?"

"Yes, my queen," said the guard.

Blanche crossed the room to stand supportively beside Evaine as she dislodged the wax with her fingernail and carefully unfolded the parchment. The note was unsigned.

Queen Evaine

The king, Wesley, and the guards found Larkin and Silas the soothsayer at a cottage in Huntington. Larkin and several mercenaries are thankfully dead, but Silas cast a spell over the king, rendering him unconscious. Wesley tried to help but was injured. The guards managed to carry them both to the safety of a stable, but mercenaries are closing in. Please come. Your touch is the only cure for our king. Wear a disguise and travel by cart, but no warriors or guards. They are watching and will know.

For the West!

Horror clawed her heart, and Evaine gasped. Was this real? A trick? Her mate had said to stay here, but the note contained so much detail. What was she to do?

"My queen?" said Blanche, taking her arm.

Evaine closed her eyes briefly, praying this would be the correct decision. "Alaric and Wesley need our help. We must wear hooded cloaks and leave now. No guards or warriors. Just us."

The elder wolf's eyes flared; for the first time, there was true panic there. Then Blanche seemed to collect herself and nodded briskly. "Of course. I'll fetch cloaks. Guard, arrange a cart at once. And several blades."

The male nodded. "Aye, mistress."

After tearing the train from her gown and changing her shoes to sturdier leather, Evaine donned the warm cloak. Then she and Blanche hurried downstairs to the courtyard, where several grim-faced guards had a cart waiting. One pointed out the swords and daggers under the bench seat.

Another stepped forward. "My queen, are you sure about this? The note could be a trick."

"Or true," she replied sharply. "There is enough detail to investigate. I'll certainly not sit idly by while my king and his squire suffer. Where is the messenger?"

"Here, madam," said a hard-eyed wolfling as he bowed awkwardly. "I'm a stablehand. The guards paid me to take you there. I know a hidden way under the city walls—the lads and I use it all the time. You'll be safe, I swear. But King Alaric needs you, he was going *gray*. And his squire has an ugly side wound."

"Leto have mercy," whispered Blanche, pulling up her cloak hood before grasping the reins of the cart horse. "My Wesley. I'll sup on their hearts."

"Willie has command of the tower," snarled Evaine, pulling up her own hood. "Now go. Take me to the king."

Despite the faint afternoon sunshine, the cold air soon burned her cheeks as the messenger led them down various alleyways and lanes and along sections of city wall. They weren't ambling, but she resisted the urge to change into wolf form and charge ahead, a truly useless endeavor when she didn't know the area. Thankfully, they soon came upon a damaged section of wall covered in canvas. The stablehand lifted it, then guided them carefully through the rubble and stone. Ahead stretched a long, unkempt-looking road seemingly following the River Dee.

"This way, madam," called the wolfling. "It's much faster to Huntington. Much less riders and carts to block us."

"Stay alert, my queen," muttered Blanche. "I'd tuck a dagger in your cloak as well."

Evaine nodded, discreetly collecting some sheathed daggers from under the seat. After handing two to Blanche, she slipped one into her bodice and attached the second to her girdle.

Gah. In her worry, had she been a bone-headed fool and leaped straight into danger?

After what seemed like a hundred miles of travel, the stablehand at last turned down a short lane. In the distance, there were several whitewashed stone buildings guarded by a wolf in Beaumont livery, who beckoned them forward.

Evaine sat up straighter, needing to see Alaric, for only holding her mate would soothe her soul. Another liveried guard took the carthorse's bridle, coaxing him to enter the stable. Unable to wait, Evaine jumped down from the cart, her gaze darting in all directions. "Where is the king?"

Blanche also dismounted. "And my young. Where is Wesley?"

"Did you really think they'd be here? Oh dear. Addled minds and soft hearts are the reason you'll both die."

Blanche gasped and Evaine spun on her heel. "*Silas?*"

The soothsayer emerged from a shadowed corner of the dusty stable holding a crossbow. "I gave you the chance to be free at Carmarthen, *duchess*. You were shrewish and threatening."

"Blanche is worse. I cannot bear the sight of either,"

added a peevish, petulant voice. Larkin!

Blanche laughed at the chamberlain. "Cwningen speaks!"

The chamberlain hissed and limped forward, clutching his blood-soaked side. "Silence, she-wolf! You always put yourself above me and Queen Theda, when you are common filth. I'll enjoy watching you and the Eastern bitch burn. Give me your hands."

"No," snapped Evaine.

There was a faint click, then Silas pointed the crossbow directly at her. "Your hands, duchess, or I will put a bolt in your belly. A *pure silver* bolt."

Goddess. Fire could kill Blanche. A silver bolt would wound Evaine, perhaps irreversibly. She would then be entirely vulnerable to beheading.

Was this how Guy Saville murdered Mother and Father? Or had he relied entirely on the Book of Lore?

Exchanging a glance with Blanche, one that warned of silence for now, Evaine held out her hands. "As you wish."

Larkin smiled, but sweat trickled from his forehead and temples as he shackled them in chains. "At last, proper obedience. The mercenaries are coming, *duchess*. Your mate will be broken with your death, just as Oliver will be broken by Blanche's, and my vengeance will be complete. Then King Guy will rule East and West, and I'll have Blackstone Castle and all the goldmines for solace. Now, both of you, sit on that hay bale."

Fury burned through Evaine, but she would kill this fool soon enough. It was the rest that terrified her. Where was Alaric? If she reached out through their fledgling bonded link, would he hear her? Would he find her in time?

Alaric. Help me.

Alaric!

CHAPTER
ELEVEN

W hen Leto was displeased, she made it painfully obvious.

Alaric rubbed his jaw as he watched the guard attempt a horseshoe repair; it was either that or he would commence destroying an entire woodland with his sword.

He'd been defeated by a damned flag, his horse had thrown a shoe and pulled up lame barely a mile from Huntington, and worst of all, his mate was vexed with him and he wasn't entirely sure why. Evaine's curt replies had stung a little, but when she'd grimaced and declined to kiss him after he'd won his sword fight, he'd known true hurt. The bone-deep hurt of rejection from the only wolf he couldn't bear rejection from. He'd grown used to Theda closing her door; everyone knew she avoided his touch. But Evaine had always loved it, any time, anywhere. Not just in bed, but casual touch like embraces or holding hands, or when he cupped her cheek.

His mate was now the center of his existence and it went far beyond friendship, affection, lust or even the soul-joining of bonded fated mates. No, this was entirely in his chest. In his heart, where all those damned emotions that he'd suppressed as a diplomat resided. The seal had been broken and they'd surged free. He could feel. He could love. And he loved Evaine.

Alaric blinked, the thought so startling he almost tripped over his own feet as the faint sound of windchimes tinkled in his ears.

Wait. *Windchimes?*

"*Evie?*" he said slowly, actually tapping his temple as the windchimes grew louder and louder. "*Evie?*"

"*Alaric!*"

Alarm surged through him at the urgency in her voice. "*What happened? Is the tower under attack?*"

"*I'm not in the tower. Blanche and I are in Huntington. We've been taken prisoner by Larkin and Silas. They locked us in a stable and have a crossbow with silver bolts. But Larkin is throwing pitch around. They are going to set the stable alight. Goddess, they've both lost their minds. But they said they want to break you.*"

Once again, that startling, ice-cold calmness draped around Alaric like another cloak. He turned to two of the guards. "Ride for the tower like your lives depend upon it. Bring all the weapons you can. I'll summon the warriors and Chester's Guard. We are returning to Huntington and going to war. Queen Evaine and Mistress Blanche have been taken and imprisoned in a stable there. GO."

The two males bolted away.

"They have Mother?" said Wesley, his face ashen.

"Yes," said Alaric, briefly gripping his squire's shoulder. "You must be braver than you've ever been. As must I."

Wesley closed his eyes, and when he opened them again, there was a certain hardness, a certain determination that said the wolfling was no more. Here was a young warrior, ready to fight. "Just tell me what to do."

Nodding in satisfaction, Alaric threw back his head and roared a call to battle. Even to his own ears the sound soared and shook the heavens, and shortly afterward came the sweet echo of wolves answering his war cry. They had heard and were on their way.

Concentrating fiercely, Alaric searched for the link to Evaine once more. "*Sweetheart, we're coming.*"

A reply came, but it was faint. "*Hurry, Alaric.*"

"Take this horse, my king," said one of the remaining guards. "I'll change and run beside you."

Never had Alaric been so nimble as he switched mounts. Then they galloped toward Huntington, uncaring of the wind and icy cold, both he and Wesley crouched low as they urged their horses on. Twice more, Alaric roared, a sound for his warriors to follow with their keen hearing. Soon they reached a small rise, one that offered a clear view of the surrounding area. Already there were wolves gathering behind him, some wearing black-and-gold livery and armed on horseback, others in wolf form prowling the grounds. The Chester Guard came from all over Cheshire and could form at a moment's notice.

Unfortunately, in the distance, he could see several lines of mercenaries. But between him and them: the stables where Evaine and Blanche were being held. Goddess. They would be at the center of the battle.

Abruptly a wolf bounded up and crouched low in deference. "My king, I bring news. There appears to be at least two hundred well-armed mercenaries, but..."

"But what?" said Alaric impatiently.

"Advancing from the rear, warriors wearing the green

and white of the Eastern Lands and flying Saville's crest. They probably marched from Sheffield."

Fury burned in his gut. Did Guy Saville lead them? Did the murdering usurper dare encroach on the Western Lands wearing the sacred ancient colors of the de Wynters? Of course he would dare. Especially with such regular, valuable notes arriving from Silas and Larkin, telling him exactly where the royal progression was, and the closest location to send Eastern warriors from.

"Share this message from me," said Alaric. "Queen Evaine and Mistress Blanche are being held captive in those stables over there. They face the threats of silver crossbow and burning; I understand pitch has already been thrown. Collect buckets and fill them from the River Dee. I want a chain stretching to swiftly extinguish flames if needed. I know this place is fairly isolated, but there may be humans around and they do not deserve to lose everything they have to fire."

"Aye, my king. One question. Are we taking prisoners for an exchange?"

"No. We will rescue the queen and Mistress Blanche, then execute every single traitor and every single enemy who dared encroach on my lands. For the West!"

"For the West!" the wolf snarled, before bounding away.

"My king," said Wesley urgently. "Can we advance on the stable yet?"

"Hold," said Alaric. "Let me see if I can link with the queen again to get further information."

Then he closed his eyes. "*Evie. Can you hear me? We are nearby, just atop a rise. I have called every guard and warrior available. They are amassing as we speak. But I need to know where you are in the stable. How many there are to kill.*"

For an endless moment he heard nothing whatsoever and sheer terror clawed his soul. Then her voice came through. *"There is a small window to my left, none other on that wall. Blanche and I are chained back to back, but our hands are in front of us, so we cannot assist each other. There only seems to be four here: Larkin, Silas, and two guards. The guards are dressed in Beaumont livery, so be wary. I understand that Larkin wishes us to burn and Silas wishes to shoot us with the crossbow if we attempt to flee. I am itching to fashion a girdle of their entrails. Larkin is having trouble with the flint. His flame keeps extinguishing, even though there is no wind or rain. Perhaps Leto watches over us."*

Alaric almost smiled. Evaine could be sweet and submissive, bold and mischievous, but he did rather enjoy her bloodthirsty streak. When this was over, she could fashion all the entrail girdles she wished. Leto willing, Guy Saville's would be one of them. *"I am sure the Blessed Goddess is watching. Tell Blanche that Wesley and I are approaching."*

"He's not hurt? The note we received said otherwise. Or was that just Larkin?"

"Just Larkin. Wesley is ready to spill blood. We are riding now."

Alaric then turned to his squire. "There are but four: Larkin, Silas, and two guards in Beaumont livery. I don't want any others to accompany us; it may cause confusion with the clothing. Is your bow and arrow ready?"

Wesley inclined his head, tapping the bow and gesturing to the nearly full quiver of arrows on his back. "Ever ready, my king."

"Our attack must be swift and deadly. The queen and your mother are chained together near the wall with one window and have had pitch poured around them."

Wesley growled. "No prisoners."

"None," replied Alaric, unsheathing his sword. "Let us ride."

They cantered toward the stable. As soon as they were close, one of the guards ran at them, brandishing his sword. Wesley felled him with an arrow to the chest. The other guard attempted to flee on foot, but Alaric rode him down, slashing his sword in an upward cut that severed the guard's spine.

Four had become two.

As they continued on around the side of the stable, flames were already flickering and smoke was starting to rise—Larkin was running with a lit torch, touching it to the wood to help the blaze along. Just as Alaric was about to dismember his former chamberlain, Wesley yelled "Look out!"

Alaric veered away, but the bolt aimed at his heart from Silas's crossbow still gouged his left arm and the burning kiss of the deadly silver made him hiss in pain. Yet now, for a short while at least, the soothsayer was unarmed. "Wesley! Free the queen and your mother. I'll tend to these two."

His squire leaped from his horse and dashed into the stable. After rendering Larkin unconscious, Alaric circled Silas. The soothsayer swiftly withdrew a small bag of blue powder, tossing the contents about and chanting.

"Too late for that," snarled Alaric, one downward cut leaving the other wolf without his left hand.

"L-Leto will save me," said Silas, his face paling as his blood spurted. Then he sank to his knees. "If I'd helped Theda when she fell, you would never have met Evaine. I did you a great service!"

"*Monster*," said Alaric, resting his blade against the soothsayer's neck.

"You cannot stop this. King Cyrus was weak and you are

weaker, always choosing treaties over battles. Accepting a human dukedom instead of waging war! That is why your line must end. Why King Guy will take the Western throne—"

The sound seemed to hang in the air as Silas' head fell to the ground with a thud, his lips forever frozen.

Sheathing his sword, Alaric then slid from his horse and sprinted toward the burning stable. "Evaine. *Evaine!*"

———

The spit and crackle of flame devouring wood assaulted her ears, smoke was stinging her eyes, but by far the worst part of being trapped in a burning stable was the rising heat.

Evaine gritted her teeth, wanting to scream in pure rage. Her first task would be killing Larkin. After that, anyone who got in her way. Poor Wesley was trying his very best to break the lock linking the chains, but he wasn't quite strong enough.

Then she heard her mate's voice, not in her head, but at the stable entrance.

"Evaine? Evaine!"

"Here!" she yelled. "Alaric!"

Her mate burst in, his clothing splattered with blood and ash. First, he took the lock from Wesley, crushing it in his fist. Then, after he freed both her and Blanche, all four ran back outside. Moments later, the roof began to collapse with a low roar, as though the fire was furious it hadn't devoured them also. The flames soared toward the sky, threatening to set the trees nearby alight, until a group of Western wolves passing buckets from the river doused it completely.

The fire had been defeated, but the war had just begun.

Unable to bear the restriction of her singed, smoke-ruined gown and cloak on her too-hot, too-sensitive skin any longer, Evaine turned to Alaric. "Can you cut off my clothing? They took my girdle dagger, but there is another in my bodice. I'll fight in wolf form. I'm much stronger this way, I don't know how to use a sword or bow."

Surprisingly, her mate didn't argue. He merely removed the hidden dagger, carefully sliced open her bodice and the ties fastening her sleeves, then held up his cloak so she could change in privacy.

Evaine kicked the fabric away, sighing in pure relief as her skin cooled in the chilly late afternoon air. Then she closed her eyes and willed herself into wolf form, whimpering a little at the change. Why was it so painful again today?

With a quick shake to clear her head, Evaine extended her claws and scratched at the fragrant earth, stretching her wolf limbs. A low groan to her right made her smile, and Evaine padded over to where Larkin lay prone on the ground, attempting to crawl further from the scene of his murderous intent.

"Chamberlain," she purred, her fangs tingling. "Leaving so soon? How unfortunate, when I have a craving for roasted rabbit."

Larkin turned onto his back—a position of submission —his arms bloodied and eyes wide. "You don't understand. Lady Theda was *mine*. The king stole her from me! I had to avenge her death. Show mercy."

Mercy?

This traitor truly thought his queen would offer leniency after all his vile acts? When he'd helped Guy Saville, tried to kill her and Blanche, and put Alaric and

Wesley and all the other brave Western wolves here at risk with this impending battle?

"No mercy for traitors," Evaine snarled, sinking her claws into his throat and ripping it out. When she looked up, the group of wolves that had extinguished the fire all bowed.

"Evaine is queen, long may she reign!" called one, and the rest cheered.

She inclined her head, then loped back to where her mate and the others waited.

Alaric was wiping blood from his sword with the edge of his cloak. "The matter is done?"

"Yes," she replied, bunting his thigh with her head. "After that taste, I'll show even less mercy to those wearing de Wynter colors against me."

Without warning, a female guard bounded around the corner in wolf form, dropping her front legs in deference. "They're charging! The mercenaries are charging with the Eastern warriors behind!"

Alaric leaped back onto his horse. "Give Mistress Blanche a sword. Wesley, onto the rise and wound as many as you can with arrows. My queen..."

"I shall be by your side, my king," she snapped, before he could be foolish and ask her to leave the battleground for her own safety. "Nowhere else."

Somehow, that made her mate grin, like she'd whispered an endearment rather than irritably scolded him. "Very well. Let us meet this foe and vanquish them utterly!"

The group scattered. Wesley rode back to the rise, collecting even more arrows from the wagons that had arrived, then set his place. Fortunately, Alaric's commanders had already organized the warriors into lines based on the weapons they held: spears at the front, swords in the middle, and archers at the rear. All those in wolf form, including Evaine, received a smear of enchanted golden clay across their fur for recognition. Apparently no one was exactly sure where the clay came from, but the pot never emptied, and it couldn't be removed until the anointed King of the Western Lands declared victory or defeat.

Alaric raised his sword and turned to his subjects. "The traitors have been executed. But our enemies still come! They dare encroach on peaceful Western Lands and think to conquer my realm. But they will die in vain. For the West! And the de Wynters!"

Then her mate threw back his head and howled, a truly blood-chilling sound. Evaine added her own howl, the two twining together so perfectly that the air crackled and blue sparks streaked across the gray sky.

"For the West and the de Wynters!" called Evaine, rising up on her hind legs and slashing her claws. "Onward!"

"Archers!" bellowed Alaric. "Fire!"

A flurry of arrows soared over their heads like a swarm of deadly brown insects, seeking out their prey with great precision and embedding in the chests and faces of the charging mercenaries. Yet even as riders fell and horses bolted from the field, still more came. Alaric called for arrows twice more, but as the mercenaries had no archers, it was clear this battle would be won by blade. Wolf against wolf.

"Spears!" barked Alaric. "Swords and claws at the ready!"

Evaine sucked in several deep breaths. Really, she should be terrified at the scent and sounds of death and violence in the air, but she was just too furious. And over-warm. Never in her life had the craving to tear another wolf limb from limb been so strong.

But before she could charge into the fray, a faint green glow from behind the Eastern line caught her eye, and Evaine froze. She would recognize that hue anywhere.

The Book of Lore.

Not wanting to alarm their side, Evaine reached out to her mate with their mind link. "*Alaric. Look north then slightly west. The green glow. It's the Book of Lore!*"

"*Are you sure?*" he replied urgently. "*I've never seen it up close.*"

"*I'm certain. If we capture that, Guy Saville has nothing. He'll be finished.*"

Alaric chuckled, a truly malevolent sound. "*Then let us capture it, my queen. I'll protect the tome, you can exact justice on the usurper.*"

"*We have ourselves a bargain,*" said Evaine, anticipation coiling in her belly as ahead of her, the Western riders with long spears charged and hurled the deadly javelins at the approaching enemy. Damn the mercenaries! How could there still be so many?

On her mate's call, all the warriors and guards with swords, including Blanche, and those in wolf form surged forward. Soon after came the first soul-shaking shriek of steel on steel. The relentless barrage of noise was disorientating at first; the thumping of hooves on dirt, the clashing of swords and shields, the growling grunts of wolves fighting, the cries of pain. How did warriors do this every day? But soon Evaine's mind cleared and she attacked her first victim, taking a chunk out of the mercenary's right shoulder and causing him to drop his sword.

Again and again she leaped and bit, ducking and weaving to avoid the swinging blades, before Alaric killed the temporarily defenseless warrior with a slash to the belly or throat. Sometimes she moved too slowly or went the wrong way; already her fur was sticky with the blood of seeping cuts. But this only fueled her rage, especially when she saw Alaric's shield occasionally drop.

"*What is wrong with your left arm?*" she demanded through their link. "*Are you hurt?*"

"*Crossbow bolt gouged it,*" her mate replied. "*Damned silver infection.*"

Gah! The longer this battle continued, the weaker his arm would become without treatment. She had to be fiercer. Not just Evaine the Bold, but Evaine the Blood-thirsty. Yet already she could feel the cruel tendrils of fatigue curling their way around her. Her cuts stung. Her limbs hurt. Her jaw ached.

Fight on, my precious cub. Fight like the de Wynter you are. We are so proud of you.

As her mother's voice danced on the air, vigor burst through Evaine. With a vengeful snarl she tore through the mercenary lines to those daring to wear the green-and-white de Wynter livery, attacking them with fang and claw in a storm of mindless savagery. Some of the warriors surrendered, throwing down their weapons and begging forgiveness from a true de Wynter. But far too many wanted her dead.

"That female's green eyes! It's Evaine de Wynter!"

"Get her! She's worth a fortune!"

"Tell King Guy to open the Book of Lore. The power will destroy her!"

Her enemies' words swirled around her like a suffocating fog and Evaine briefly lifted her head to study the battlefield. Most of the fighting raged behind her, but ahead, surely not more than a quarter mile, astride a horse and watching proceedings like the festering turd coward he was: Guy Saville.

She growled, the sound emanating from the depths of her soul. Somehow she just knew the usurper had seen her, for he lifted the Book of Lore above his head and pointed it. A bolt of green lightning shot from the tome and Evaine knew a moment of true despair at her failure, bracing herself for paralyzing agony.

Except the bolt passed through her with no more than a brief sting. Guy bellowed in rage and shot a second bolt. Again, it did nothing.

Shock almost sent Evaine to her knees. As the Book always remained at Ashcross Castle, she had never considered that it might lose its tremendous force outside the Eastern Lands. Did anyone know that? Guy Saville certainly didn't!

"*Alaric!*" she cried, through their mind link. "*Take him now! Guy Saville is vulnerable in the Western Lands! Alaric, can you hear me? Where are you?*"

———

Alaric's entire world had reduced solely to instinct; anything else just reminded him how badly his arm hurt. Silver infections were another Hera-inflicted torment, burning into flesh like a brand and poisoning the blood. To treat it, every Western healer carried wild garlic and white willow bark for pain relief and to soothe inflammation, also vials of enchanted water from the spring at Taff's Well. But it really was a matter of time. If silver got into vital organs like the heart or lungs, unlike any other ailment, the damage was irreversible. He would be bedridden the rest of his life.

Right now he couldn't even examine his flesh. Apart from the constant danger, he was covered in so much blood he wasn't entirely sure which was his and which had spurted from his enemies as he severed limbs or removed innards. The grass had become red and slippery, and on several occasions he'd almost lost his footing. Chester's body wagons would be busy this night; thankfully the village's isolation meant few humans would witness the bloodbath.

A low battle cry came from his right, and Alaric turned wearily, raising his shield just in time to block a strong blow from a mercenary. He immediately countered with an upward cut, dislodging the other wolf's sword, then gutting him with a straight thrust.

How many more? Surely he'd already killed hundreds.

"Evaine," he muttered aloud. "My arm *hurts*."

Where was his mate? The last he knew, Evaine had been merrily slashing and biting her way through their enemy. But although he could see Blanche, her gown cut to above her knees, and fighting as skillfully as anyone, his mate was nowhere to be found. "Evie?"

Goddess. Was she hurt? Had she retreated for safety? Had she grown weary of his failure to defeat the Eastern warriors and left him?

Another wave of agony surged down Alaric's arm, his shield feeling heavier than an anvil. Without the leather straps tying it to him, it would be impossible to hold up. Yet a heartbeat later, he almost forgot that wound as fire slashed across his lower thigh.

A silver blade!

Alaric coughed, his whole body crushed in a vise of pain as the grinning Eastern captain circled him. Perhaps this was it. Perhaps he was destined to perish on the battlefield rather than grow old with Evaine. But damn it, he would go down fighting. "Is that your best? I've seen cubs with more skill."

His enemy hissed at the insult. "I'll enjoy presenting a royal head to King Guyyyy...wretched little turd!"

Blinking in confusion, Alaric tried to clear his blurry vision. Had Wesley truly appeared, a too-heavy longsword swaying awkwardly in his grip, and sliced the captain's arse?

"Get away from my king," said Wesley fiercely.

Their enemy laughed then swung his sword horizontally, easily dislodging Wesley's weapon and cutting the squire's shoulder. However, the diversion gave Alaric the opportunity to strike, and he lunged with his blade. The captain howled at the deep cut to his side, yet managed to raise his shield and block Alaric's next blow. At the sickening impact of metal on metal, another jolt of agony passed through Alaric and he staggered back before sinking to one knee.

"Give my regards to Leto," bellowed the captain. But just as he lifted his sword high to deliver the death blow, a snarling gray beast came hurtling through the air toward him like a battering ram, knocking him to the ground and slashing his throat.

Alaric beamed even as he slumped to the grass. "Evie," he said. "You came back."

She licked his face. "I never left. And the battle is won; Guy Saville's forces are trying to flee!"

"I love you so much," he slurred. Then everything went black.

When he opened his eyes, Alaric frowned at the murky darkness. Where was he? There was no pain in his arm and thigh, or anywhere for that matter. In fact, he felt rested and refreshed which was entirely suspicious. Had he succumbed to silver poisoning and been beheaded? Had he risen to the stars?

"Am I dead?" he mumbled.

"No, you're not dead. But what kind of right royal arse fights on with silver poisoning? I should have dragged you to a healer myself. You don't have the sense of a turnip, Alaric," said the sweetest scold in the Western Lands, now in human form and wearing a borrowed robe.

"My mate," he said lovingly.

Evaine huffed out a breath but she was stroking his hair and holding his hand like she'd been fretting. "I'll send in the Chester healer to examine you again—she's very experienced. Wesley is pacing the hallway. Oh, and we're in a cottage because no one wanted to risk transporting you. There are hundreds of guards outside, I believe Blanche is in command. Do not *dare* move."

"Yes, my queen," Alaric replied, as meekly as he could.

As soon as she departed the small, simply furnished room, Wesley dashed in, his expression one of pure relief. "Everyone was terrified. They thought you might die. Mother hauled you to safety, it was the strangest thing, like for a short time she had the strength of a goddess. Then she demanded a flagon of wine, drank the entire thing, and more warriors fell in love with her. UGH."

Alaric suppressed a smile at the details, far too glad to witness the return of playful Wesley. "Let us speak of events on the battlefield."

His squire flushed. "I know I was only supposed to fire arrows. But I had none left and that Eastern captain had a silver sword! Then he wounded your thigh, so I picked up a sword from the ground and sliced him. I wanted to help..."

"You saved your king's life, Wesley. You are as brave as any warrior and a skilled archer."

"Awww, well, you know," said the squire as he squirmed, his ears bright pink. "Couldn't let anything happen when you have, ah, special duties tomorrow."

Alaric frowned. "What? There aren't any meetings or ceremonies."

Wesley actually laughed. "Ohhhhhhh, my king, for the first time I know something you don't! The queen has been out of sorts all day, yes? Irritable, too hot?"

"Being confined to a tower, tricked by a note, taken prisoner, then having to escape a burning stable and fight a vicious battle would make anyone irritable," he replied, narrowing his gaze at the young wolf's glee.

His squire kneeled beside the bed. "My king, everyone noticed. And we are so joyful for you both."

"What in Leto's name are you prattling about?" Alaric said, genuinely baffled.

"Mother said this always happens to a mated she-wolf the day before she goes into her breeding heat," Wesley whispered. "Because it's the queen's first time, she might not realize either!"

Alaric bolted upright in bed as a storm of emotions battered him. Like so many males in his pack, soon he would know the sweet exhaustion of easing his mate's need. Evie could conceive. They might have *cubs* by May.

Tears burned his eyes and he coughed to clear the boulder in his throat. Fated mate didn't begin to describe the way she had turned his existence of cold, bleak duty into one of fierce lust and tenderness. Companionship and warmth and loyalty. With Evie at his side, together they could achieve anything. His queen. His mate. His love.

"Indeed," Alaric said softly, trying not to grin like a nodcock and failing utterly. "Send in the healer, would you?"

Wesley bowed, his eyes twinkling. "Yes, my king."

When the she-wolf bustled in, Alaric inclined his head. "I thank you for your care."

The brown-haired healer glared at him. "Please do not risk your life and health with silver poisoning again, my king."

"I swear," he replied solemnly. "I'm feeling surprisingly well, considering."

Her lips twitched. "As well as a generous dosing of enchanted water, I blended a marshmallow ointment for the wound sites, put apple cider vinegar compresses on your feet, and dripped dandelion tea down your throat. You're going to need all your strength for the coming week."

Alaric blushed. "Goddess, everyone really does know."

"Aye. The news spread faster than wildfire. How could it not? Your true fated mate going into her breeding heat offers the chance of heirs to the Western throne!"

"And, ah, what is best for the queen?" he asked hesitantly.

The healer nodded approvingly. "A cool bath tonight. Plenty of food and drink. And I mean *plenty*. Like you're feeding an entire castle. You'll both be ravenous. Oh, and my king, you might be unaware, but if the queen conceives, she will change to wolf form shortly afterward and remain that way until after she delivers. That is how you know."

Grateful beyond measure for the plain-spoken information, Alaric nodded. "Thank you again. See Mistress Blanche, she'll pay in gold for your services."

"Much obliged, my king," said the healer, bobbing a curtsy then departing.

Soon after, Evaine appeared in the doorway, tearing into a juicy slab of rare beef. "So, I'm a little confused why every wolf in the area is offering me food, but I like it. What did the healer say?"

Goddess. Whether in human or wolf form, his mate truly was the most beautiful creature on this earth.

Alaric smiled as he stood. "She didn't exactly say 'you haven't the sense of a turnip, Alaric' but the sentiment was there."

Evaine hesitated. "About that..."

"No, my queen. You were entirely correct. I put myself and others in danger, and if it weren't for you and Wesley, I would have perished. I am indeed fortunate that my mate would rip out a throat for me. Perhaps you love me a little?" he finished hopefully, because he loved her so completely.

"A *little*?" she snapped, her eyes blazing. "I love you more than the moon and the stars and the sun. You fill my thoughts during the day and my dreams at night. I cannot imagine a world without my king. And you are *my* king. Mine. I will sleep and rut with you, dine and hunt with you, embrace your friends and shred your enemies. But most of all, I'll love and cherish you. Forever."

"Then Leto has blessed us both," he replied, marching over to take her into his arms. "You are everything to me, Evie."

She sighed happily and cuddled against him, then took another bite of meat. "I am rather relieved you wanted an embrace and not my beef. That would have ended badly for you."

Alaric laughed. "Now, my beloved. About tomorrow..."

EPILOGUE

There were truly no words to describe the sheer incessant *need* that came with a royal she-wolf's breeding heat.

Evaine moved restlessly on the bed, whimpering a little as the inferno within her began to rise again. Nothing could ease her except a screaming release. Although she gained a short respite each time Alaric used his tongue or fingers, the only time her blood cooled long enough to rest was after her mate's cock had locked inside her, flooding her cunt with seed.

They'd not left this bedchamber in days. While all their subjects had been ordered to stay at least fifty feet away from Wolf's Gate Tower to lessen the impact of her heat on them, Blanche had recruited a huge number of local wolves to act as temporary servants. They took turns bringing fresh food and wine, bathing water, messages, and linen, and left them outside the chamber door. It seemed the Cestrians were thrilled that such an important and special event had occurred in their town, and they all wanted to say that they'd served.

Evaine tried not to ponder the fact that every wolf in the

Western Lands knew she was in her heat and that she and Alaric were rutting like wild beasts—it would be far too embarrassing. This was simply a sacrifice that came with being royal: certain aspects of your life would never be private, and a breeding heat which might result in a prince for the Western throne was one of them.

"Alaric," she whispered. "I'm too hot."

"One moment, sweetheart. I'll get some fresh cool water," said her mate, as he climbed off the bed and ambled over to the door.

Evaine licked her lips at the delectable sight. His perfect arse already carried several bite marks of appreciation, and his back was covered in scratches. There were, however, a few unblemished inches. She certainly needed to add to her canvas. "Hurry, my mate."

Alaric glanced over his shoulder and winked. When he opened the chamber door to collect the fresh supplies: a bucket of herbed water, jug of wine, and a tray of sliced meats and honey cakes, he deliberately bent right over.

Oh, her king wished to tease? Evaine's mouth watered, the inner flame rising higher and higher, and she growled. Then she sprang from the bed and walked to the coolest corner of the chamber, the one where they ate and bathed. It was far too warm for her in front of the fire.

"Sponge me," Evaine purred, running her hands over her breasts and tweaking her nipples.

Alaric's eyes glittered as he approached. First, he set down the food and wine, then he continued toward her with the herbed water. At the first touch of the deliciously cold liquid to her overheated skin, Evaine sighed in pleasure. But as he ran the sponge over her flesh, there were certain areas such as her back and legs that he gently scrubbed, whereas he offered no more than the briefest touch to her swollen nipples and aching center. Wicked wolf.

Evaine growled a warning. In response, he soaked the sponge and crushed it on her shoulder, allowing the water to flow down over her breasts and drip from her nipples. Then he bent her back over his strong arm, lapping and sucking the water away.

Ah. Much better.

She moaned at the deliciously rough tugging on her nipples, threading her fingers through Alaric's hair and holding him in place. But it wasn't nearly enough to sate her, and soon her hips circled, trying to find something, anything to rub against.

"Poor sweetheart," he murmured. "You need to spend again, don't you?"

Evaine cried out in gratitude as he slid the sponge down over her stomach to her mound, then rubbed back and forth against her pleasure bud. As a loving mate he didn't make her wait, dropping the sponge on the floor and replacing it with his hand, penetrating her sheath with two fingers and plunging them deep. Her release was shockingly swift, and she screamed in delight as his thumb pressed her pleasure bud to prolong it. However, unlike all the previous occasions in the week, it didn't start a gentle cooling wave within her. The inferno merely climbed higher.

"Alaric," she said in panicked confusion. "It's not stopping. Goddess, please. Again."

Her mate immediately scooped her up in his arms and carried her over to the bed. "My tongue?"

"Yes," Evaine begged, spreading her thighs wide for him.

Alaric growled, the low rumble provoking even more honey to flow from her center. As he dragged his tongue through her petal-soft folds, she moaned, eagerly grinding against his chin and coating his mouth in her wetness. A second release burst through her and she cried out, bucking on the bed. And yet again, it wasn't enough to douse the flame.

"Evie?" said Alaric, his brow furrowing as he rested his chin on her inner thigh.

Evaine writhed on the bed, her fingernails near-slashing the sheets. "Please," she gasped, the inferno actually painful now. "I need you inside me. Seed. Give me seed. Hurry. *Hurry.*"

He took his engorged cock in hand, rubbing the head against her slickness to fully wet it, then he entered her, slowly but relentlessly. "There, shhh, here you go sweetheart. Take it all."

Tilting her hips and wrapping her legs around his flanks, Evaine pulled him close to ensure he was as deep inside her as possible. "Harder, my king. *Harder.*"

With a feral snarl, Alaric slowly withdrew, then thrust brutally forward. Again and again he pounded into her and it was so perfect, so necessary, that Evaine could only chant his name as she clutched at his shoulders, willing him on, willing him to quench the unbearable fire threatening to consume her. Abruptly her fangs elongated, and she turned her head slightly and sank them into the curve of his shoulder.

It was like being struck by lightning. Stunning pleasure engulfed Evaine and her scream of pure ecstasy twined with Alaric's roar as they knotted together, his cock expanding and her cunt contracting around his length, milking him of seed until it gushed inside her greedy sheath, filling her and filling her. At last she found blessed cool relief and when her mate slumped down on top of her, she nuzzled him, licking at the small puncture wound and crooning nonsense words in his ear.

Eventually, Alaric carefully rolled onto his back, so she lay on his chest. His hand began stroking her sweat-covered shoulders, and it was so soothing her eyes grew heavy and her body relaxed, her inner walls slowly releasing their vise-like grip on his cock. When it at last slipped free, Evaine flopped onto her side, grimacing a little at the soreness between her legs. Yet there was another sensation as well, a new, odd tingling in her lower belly.

"Alaric," she whispered, pressing her hand to her abdomen. "Something is happening. I can feel it. I think...I think I might have conceived."

He covered her hand with his, gently cradling her belly, and the awe and wonder on his face brought tears to her eyes. "Really? I mean, I hoped beyond measure...cubs from my Evie would be a gift above any other."

Without warning, Evaine's body bucked then curled, and she changed into wolf form with a startled yelp.

Goddess!

Her mind still whirling, she rested her muzzle on her mate's thigh. But wanting some part of this to be private, Evaine reached out through their mind link. *"Well. I believe the question has been answered. I suppose we must announce it?"*

Alaric shrugged as he tenderly smoothed her fur. *"They'll know soon enough. I must also warn you: the blessing ceremony for the birth of a royal heir requires the Western crowns to be hauled out of the Treasury again. And I probably cannot deny Rowan his moment in the sun a second time. No halting him mid-speech to hasten the bedding."*

"*Ugh, those crowns,*" said Evaine, laughing reluctantly. "*But what if I need to be bedded?*"

"*Then you would have to beg most prettily, my queen,*" said Alaric, his eyes glinting. Oh indeed, her king was the most contented male in Wolfdom.

She rolled her eyes, then yawned. "*A she-wolf beg? Ha. Now, pet me some more. I desire to lie here alone with you for as long as possible.*"

"*As you wish. We have so many adventures ahead.*"

Evaine sighed contentedly at his touch, although her joy at impending motherhood was tinged with sadness and anxiety, too. Mother and Father could only watch from the stars. And somewhere, Isabel, Cecily and Lucan were still running. Still hiding. Still in terrible danger, because while Guy Saville had lost the battle, the war for the Eastern throne continued. There would always be more mercenaries. Someday soon, the usurper would return, even stronger than before.

Please, Leto. I beg thee...wherever they are, keep my sisters and brother safe.

Also by Nicola Davidson

<u>Regency full length</u>

Wickedly Wed series

Duke in Darkness (#1)

The Best Marquess (#2)

Prince of Scandal (#3)

The London Lords series

To Love a Hellion (#1)

Rake to Riches (#2)

Tempting the Marquess (#3)

<u>Regency novellas</u>

Fallen trilogy

Surrender to Sin (#1)

The Devil's Submission (#2)

The Seduction of Viscount Vice (#3)

Surrey SFS quintet

My Lady's Lover (#1)

To Tame a Wicked Widow (#2)

My Lord, Lady, and Gentleman (#3)

At His Lady's Command (#4)

A Very Surrey SFS Christmas (#5)

Surrey SFS - The Complete Series boxset

Regency Menage

A Rake, His Patron, & Their Muse (#1)

An Earl, His Valet, & Their Wife (#2)

Regency Standalones

Seven Sinful Nights

Duke for Hire

Her Virgin Duke

Mistletoe Mistress

Joy to the Earl

Once Upon a Promise

Medieval Scotland

Glennoe Highlanders

Wicked Passions (#1)

Her Wicked Highlander (#2)

Scandalous Passions

Tudor novellas

His Forbidden Lady

One Forbidden Knight

Paranormal

Medieval Wolf Kings

Wolf Duke (#1)

Contemporary

Ladies First (erotic short stories)

ABOUT THE AUTHOR

USA Today bestselling author **Nicola Davidson** worked for many years in media and government communications, but hasn't looked back since she decided writing erotic historical romance was infinitely more fun. When not chained to a computer, she can be found ambling along one of New Zealand's beautiful beaches, cheering on the All Blacks rugby team, history geeking on the internet, or daydreaming. If this includes dessert—even better!

Her books have appeared in *USA Today*, *NPR*, and *Entertainment Weekly*.

Keep up with Nicola's news on Twitter (@NicolaMDavidson) Facebook (Nicola Davidson—Author) Instagram (@NicolaDauthor) or her website www.nicola-davidson.com

www.ingramcontent.com/pod-product-compliance
Lightning Source LLC
Chambersburg PA
CBHW022137240626
47153CB00007B/2405